Mrs. Entwhistle

By Doris Reidy

Also by Doris Reidy

Every Last Stitch

Five for the Money

DEDICATION

To my children, by birth and by marriage

ACKNOWLEDGEMENTS

Thanks to Robin Achille for the cover photograph, and to Josh Langston for cover design. Thanks to the generous readers who spent hours with this manuscript, catching my mistakes and making valuable suggestions.

Mrs. Entwhistle Buys a Car

One of the worst days of her life was when her son took her car away. She didn't say that lightly, for Mrs. Entwhistle had had some bad days in her seventy-eight years. There was the day of Floyd's heart attack. The day she'd witnessed that horrible wreck on the interstate. The time Tommy got hit by a car, and she was so scared she couldn't get her breath, but it turned out his only injury was a broken arm. Awful days, every one of them, but this ranked right up there with them.

Driving meant freedom. She could get in her big Buick and go to the drugstore to get her pills whenever she needed to. She could get her hair done and visit her best friend and go to the library. Lord knows, she wasn't planning to drive to Florida, she reflected bitterly. So why did Tommy have to get so bossy and officious and tell her she wasn't safe on the road anymore, and to hand over her keys. Now. Please. And Diane just sat there nodding.

They'd both appeared unexpectedly at her door on a Saturday afternoon, looking sheepish but determined.

Choosing to sit in the front room instead of the kitchen to give their visit extra weight, she supposed, they settled in for the kill.

Just because she'd had a couple—well, three—little fender-benders in the last year or two. Okay, in the last six months. Still, those accidents could have happened to a person of any age. That stop sign, for instance, was all covered over with kudzu. How was she supposed to guess it was there? When she backed into another car at Kroger's, it was just a kiss between bumpers; you could hardly see the dent. That rude, screechy woman had gone on and on about thousands of dollars for a brand-new car and now look! People shouldn't pay so much for cars anyway. A Ford or Chevy was good enough for anybody. She only drove the Buick because that's what Floyd left her when he died.

The last accident, she was prepared to admit, was more serious. She'd been looking down to get a tissue from her purse and wham, she smacked right into the car ahead of her. Got a big goose egg on her forehead that turned into a black eye. The other driver was polite enough, but he kept repeating over and over in a most tiresome manner that he was just sitting there at a traffic light, minding his own business, and pow! She'd declined an ambulance and accepted a ticket, which she paid and hoped nobody would find out. But, of course, her nosy children knew all about it. Mrs. Entwhistle felt cross with them. More than cross: disappointed and maybe a little bit heart-broken.

She wasn't one to go down without a fight. She told Tommy and Diane that teenage drivers with their crazy speeding caused more serious accidents than senior citizens; she'd read that somewhere. She pointed out that nobody forbade them to drive. Diane countered that teenager drivers keep getting better, whereas older folks…Her mother's glare could still stop Diane in her tracks.

Mrs. Entwhistle bargained, promising to only drive close to home.

"All your accidents happened within a mile or two of home," Tommy said.

She blustered. "Who do you think you are, telling me what I can and can't do? I am still your mother." They were unmoved.

She reminded them of the inconvenience to themselves: "You'll have to get time off work for my doctor appointments and take me grocery shopping on your precious Saturdays."

"We'll work it out. We'll have a schedule," Diane replied.

To her shame, she pleaded. "Please, don't make me a prisoner in my own house."

Diane wavered then, but that Tommy, he was hard as a rock. "No, Mother, we won't let you hurt yourself or someone else. It's time to stop driving."

He drove her Buick away, and that was that.

But he'd neglected to deprive her of her perfectly valid driver's license. Certainly, she didn't wish to hurt anyone and she didn't intend to. But what she did intend to do was keep driving. She had money in savings. Mrs. Entwhistle would simply buy herself a car.

~*~

The first thing to figure out was how to get to a car dealership now that she couldn't drive there. A resident of suburbia all her life, Mrs. Entwhistle had never ridden on a city bus. Not that there were any bus lines in her neighborhood. Taxis were expensive and you didn't know exactly how much they cost until the driver told you, because who could read all that fine print on the door? Maybe she'd ask her best friend, Maxine, to take her. Her children hadn't lifted her driving privileges. Yet. Mrs. Entwhistle dialed the phone.

"Hello?"

"Max, it's Cora. Are you busy?"

"No, not a bit, just sitting here watching the birds at my feeder."

"Any good ones?"

"I think I saw a red-tail hawk. It wasn't at the feeder, but I heard a whole lot of squawking and way up in the tree, I saw an awfully big bird. Couldn't see it real well, but I bet that's what it was."

"Yes, probably. Listen, Max, I was wondering if I could ask a big favor."

"Sure, honey, what is it?"

"I need a ride to the Ford dealer out on the four-lane."

"Did your car break down?"

"No, not exactly. What it is, Tommy and Diane decided I can't drive any more. They took my car away."

"No! They did not!"

"But they did. And gave me a big lecture on how

4

I'm a danger to myself and others. That's what they said: a danger to myself and others. I never would have believed that I raised children who could be so disrespectful and ugly-acting."

"Now, Cora, don't get in a fuss. Children think they know it all and we know nothing, no matter what age they are. Why, your driving's just fine. You've had a couple of little boo-boos but no real harm done."

"So, will you take me to the car place? I'm going to get me a new car."

"Why, sure, I will. Won't that be fun! A new car."

~*~

When Maxine tapped her car horn in the driveway at ten the next morning, Mrs. Entwhistle emerged from her house promptly. She wore what she thought of as her marryin' and buryin' suit, which she'd livened up for today's important transaction with a bright pink scarf. She felt nervous. Floyd had always handled big things like car-buying. In fact, he was such a ferocious bargainer that Mrs. Entwhistle refused to accompany him on car-buying missions. It was too embarrassing. The resulting purchases were often not to her liking, but it was a man's place to buy cars and he knew best. Now she was stepping into an unfamiliar arena, but only because she had to. Thanks to her kids.

"Cora, look there. The carnival's in town," Maxine said as they neared the fairground. "Let's go in just for a minute and see if that fortune teller from last year is still there. She told me some really good stuff."

"What?"

"I don't exactly remember, but it was good. Do you mind if we run in and see?"

"You're the driver," Mrs. Entwhistle said agreeably, although she was thinking she'd never done such a thing as visit a fortune teller in her life. But Maxine was a free spirit and that was one of things she liked about her.

There weren't many cars in the parking lot at that early hour, enabling Maxine to maneuver her enormous Lincoln Navigator into a conveniently wide spot. She'd picked out that car herself, one of the first things she did after her husband died. It might just be a tad too big for Max to handle easily, since she sat so low in the driver's seat she could hardly see over the steering wheel. *But it was her choice, and let it be an example for me,* Mrs. Entwhistle thought, as she struggled down from the high seat. *If Max can do it, I can do it.*

The ladies set out on the midway, resolutely ignoring the bewitching aroma of funnel cakes. They had walked the entire length and Mrs. Entwhistle's feet were protesting – she was wearing her good shoes, after all – when they finally came to a tent set off by itself.

"Madame Esmeralda the Magnificent," read the banner over the door. No one was stirring and the place looked deserted, but Maxine was not easily deterred.

"Yoo-hoo!" she called, poking her head inside the tent. "Madame Esmeralda, are you there? Are you open?"

Draperies at the back of the tent stirred and a tousled woman wearing a bedraggled housecoat appeared. "I'm open now," she said, around a huge yawn. "You ladies here for a reading?"

"You're not Madame Esmeralda. I saw her last

year, and you're not her," Max said, her disappointment making her more blunt than usual.

"Madame Esmeraldas come and go," the woman said. "I'm Madame Esmeralda this year. Do you or don't you want your fortunes told?"

"Well. I don't know, now. I thought you'd be the real Madame Esmeralda. What do you think, Cora?"

"We walked all this way. You might as well."

"Are you not going to?"

"Oh, I don't think so. I really don't believe in that stuff. No offense," Mrs. Entwhistle added, with an apologetic glance at Madame Esmeralda.

"None taken," Madame said. She motioned to Maxine. "Please come and sit down at the table and let me consult the spirits. And that will be five dollars."

Maxine rummaged through all the pockets in her pocket book, finally extracting the requisite bill, and then settled herself in the small chair at the table. Madame Esmeralda bent low over the cloudy globe.

"The spirits are stirring," she intoned. "I see the figure of a small animal - is it a dog?"

"Yes! That's Jingo, he died last spring."

"Jingo wants me to tell you that he is happy in his heavenly home and is waiting for you."

"Awww. Bless his heart, I miss him."

Madame Esmeralda gazed some more, biting back another yawn. "You will get a new dog," she finally said, "and it will be an even better dog than Jingo. He says that's okay."

7

Max nodded eagerly. Mrs. Entwhistle knew she'd been thinking about getting a puppy, or maybe an older rescue dog.

"And I see a...wait, who's getting a new car?"

"Why, I am," Mrs. Entwhistle said. "We're on our way to the car place right now."

"Hmmmm. Not a good idea," Madame Esmeralda said flatly. "I see great danger and it has something to do with a new car. The spirits are not always plain."

"You sound just like my children," Mrs. Entwhistle said. "I can drive as well as anyone. Mind your own business and tell the spirits to mind theirs. No offense."

"Again, none taken," Madam said, "but I'm not kidding, I really did see something about an accident or something bad, and it involved a car."

"Well, thank you very much. I guess you want five dollars from me, now," Mrs. Entwhistle said in an icy voice.

"Nope, that one's on the house," Madame replied.

After more predictions about sudden wealth and the possibility of a remarriage for Maxine, the ladies took their leave of Madame Esmeralda and hiked the long way back to the car.

"I might get another dog, but I don't think I'll remarry, though," Maxine said thoughtfully. "Once was plenty, you know?"

~*~

The Ford sedans were lined up in rows in front of the dealership. They sparkled in the sunlight like multi-

8

colored gems. Maxine parked the Lincoln and she and Mrs. Entwhistle approached the front door. Inside, a huddle of men in suits and ties were laughing uproariously. As if that wasn't intimidating enough, all the men looked around at their entrance and fell silent, as if someone had flipped the "off" switch. Feeling like interlopers who'd just spoiled a good time, the ladies paused uncertainly.

A very young man detached himself from the huddle and approached them.

"Good morning, ladies, may I help you?"

"Yes, I'd like to look at cars," Mrs. Entwhistle said.

"I see. Will your husband be joining you?"

"I hope not. He's been in the grave for seven years now."

"Oh, sorry, I just thought…I meant…usually…never mind. What can I show you today?"

"I want to see your cheapest Ford sedan with an automatic transmission." Mrs. Entwhistle could drive a stick-shift, Floyd had taught her, but she'd be darned if she would, now that the choice was up to her. "And I want green," she added.

"I think we have just the thing," the young man said. "I'm John Mackey, by the way."

"The same Mackey that's on the sign?"

"That's my Dad. I'm Junior, but he's taught me a lot about cars and I'm sure I can help you."

John ushered them out into the car lot and led them to a forest green, four-door sedan. It had fancy chrome wheels – "mag wheels," John said - which Mrs. Entwhistle knew would be a bugger to keep clean, but the green paint shone with a beautiful intensity that won her heart.

"That's the one, I want that one," she said.

"Well, don't you want to drive it first?" John asked.

"Oh, yes, of course, I should drive it," Mrs. Entwhistle said, looking at Maxine doubtfully.

"Go on, now, Cora, let's just take a little spin and see how it feels to you."

"Uh, do you - you do have a driver's license?" John asked.

"I certainly do, young man," Mrs. Entwhistle replied, giving him the glare she'd so often directed successfully at her own children. It worked on him, too.

With no further chat about licenses, they piled into the car, Mrs. Entwhistle behind the wheel, John beside her in the front seat, and Maxine in the back. After adjusting the mirrors and pulling up the seat so that John's knees were jack-knifed against the dashboard, Mrs. Entwhistle turned the key in the ignition and slowly, slowly, backed out of the parking space. She crept through the car lot and paused for long moments at the entrance to the highway, looking left, then right, then left, then right. Finally, with no cars in sight in either direction, she pulled out at a dignified pace.

"She'll go a little faster," John said.

Mrs. Entwhistle pressed on the gas and the green car leapt forward, snapping their heads back. "Oops, sorry," she said, "it's got more juice than my old car had."

Now that she'd speeded up, the car felt great. The tires hummed over the roadway, the large windshield gave her a panoramic view and the new seat hit her back in just the right place. Her confidence grew.

"Oh, I like this car!" she said. "I'm going to buy it, for sure. How much is it?"

John quoted a price and glanced apologetically at Mrs. Entwhistle. But she was unfazed.

"I'll take it," she said.

"Really? Don't you want to, maybe, bargain a little bit? Talk about trade-in and all that? That's kind of how it works."

"No, I don't believe in that bargaining stuff. If that's the price, then that's the price. I'm sure you wouldn't cheat me." She peered over at John. "I have the money, you know."

"The road! Watch the road! Okay, that's better. Sorry I yelled. I'd love to sell you this car, but…are you sure?"

"Yes, young man, I'm sure."

"Okay, then. I guess we should head back to the dealership."

"Where can I make a right turn? I don't make left turns."

"Do you make U-turns?"

"Certainly not."

They drove on. None of the right turns looked suitable to Mrs. Entwhistle. She felt she'd know a safe-looking right turn when she saw one, and she hadn't seen one yet. She swerved to the right at every street to check it out, and then swerved back into her lane.

"Cora." Maxine's voice sounded strange. "Cora, I need to stop. I'm feeling kind of...oh, no!"

Mrs. Entwhistle hit the brakes and came to a lurching stop as the unmistakable odor of vomit filled the car. Maxine opened her door into traffic and the air was torn by the angry blast of a horn. She stumbled out onto the pavement and bent double, retching. John seemed to be paralyzed. Mrs. Entwhistle climbed out from behind the wheel, also into traffic, provoking another horn blast, and helped Maxine over to the side of the road.

"Now, just sit right down on the ground, Max. Here, wipe your chin a little bit. Why, I didn't know you were feeling sick."

"It was the swerving, and being in the back seat," Maxine said huskily, "I just suddenly came over hot and cold and then...I'm so sorry about messing up the car."

"Don't you worry one bit about that. I'm sure John will clean it up."

John was out of the car, too, mopping at his forehead with a white handkerchief and looking like he might throw up himself. He didn't appear to be capable of cleaning much of anything.

"Take your handkerchief and get up as much of that vomit as you can," Mrs. Entwhistle instructed him. At his appalled look, she said, "Then just throw that hankie away. Do you want to ride with that smell?"

They rolled down all the windows and Mrs. Entwhistle directed John to sit in the back so Maxine could have the front seat. His suggestion that he drive was met with a determined shake of the head. "I'm perfectly capable," Mrs. Entwhistle said. "I just need to find a good right turn."

~*~

"Max, would a Co-Cola help you feel better?"

"I believe it would, Cora, it sounds good."

By now they were far out of town on a sparsely populated stretch of highway. They passed plenty of side roads, but none that Mrs. Entwhistle thought looked promising. There were no restaurants or drive-ins on the right, the only side Mrs. Entwhistle would consider. In vain did John suggest from the back seat that maybe it was time for them to head back. Mrs. Entwhistle ignored him and drove steadily onward. Finally, she spotted a Sonic drive-in off to the right, and immediately braked for a sharp right turn, incurring the wrath of the driver behind her. She drove the short distance to the restaurant, pulled into a space and reached out for the speaker.

"Oops! That should have been fastened down better."

John blanched at the sound of metal scraping green paint as Mrs. Entwhistle dropped the speaker down the side of the car. She reeled it in by the cord, bumping all the way up, and pressed the button.

"One Co-Cola, and I believe I'll have a chocolate milkshake. Driving sure makes a person feel empty and I don't remember that we had lunch. John, did you want something?"

"No, ma'am, no thank you. I don't feel so good myself. The smell back here…"

"Okay, then." Into the speaker, she said, "Just bring us the milkshake and Co-Cola."

"Mrs. Entwhistle, now that you've finally made that right turn, it's really time we went back," John said. "I was supposed to meet my…my friend for lunch. She didn't answer when I called to tell her I couldn't make it. She's not good about checking her messages. I expect she'll think I stood her up. She'll be pretty mad."

"Why, of course, John. Just let us drink these and we'll go right back. You should have said you had a date. Is it serious?"

"Maybe, on my part. I don't think it is on hers. She's got lots of men after her, she can have her pick."

"Well, she couldn't do better than you. Don't you think so, Max?"

"Absolutely. He's a good-looking young man. You are, John. And well-spoken, too."

"Yes, and a hard worker with good prospects. Prospects can't get any better than your daddy owning the company," Mrs. Entwhistle said. The ladies laughed companionably. "I guess you'll always drive a good car, too."

"Yes, Dad likes me to drive the latest models; he thinks it's good advertising."

"So there you are: good-looking, well-spoken, hard-working, good prospects and a nice car. You don't have to take a back seat to anybody alive, John Mackey. You're a regular dreamboat. That girl is lucky you'd have her."

Mrs. Entwhistle put the car in reverse, forgetting to wait for removal of the tray on which their drinks had been

14

served. It fell with a clang when the tire rode up over the curb as she backed out.

As she approached the highway, Mrs. Entwhistle came to a full stop. She looked at oncoming traffic long and hard, letting several slow-moving cars pass, and then suddenly shot across the highway onto the southbound lane. Screeching tires and the blasting air-horn of an enormous truck made them all jump.

"Swanee!" she said. "Where did he come from?"

"Cora, maybe we ought to hurry just a little. We have to get home before it gets dark; you know I can't see to drive at night," Maxine said.

Mrs. Entwhistle dutifully pressed down on the gas, gripping the wheel with white knuckles as the speedometer climbed to thirty, forty, fifty, sixty. John shut his eyes and prayed aloud softly: "I've tried to live a good life, Lord, please don't let me die today."

"Truck! Look out!" Maxine screamed. Looming large before them, the signs on the rear of a dump truck hauling gravel warned Stay Back 50 Feet and Not Responsible for Flying Objects. As if on cue, a largish rock flew from the load and smashed into their windshield. Mrs. Entwhistle hit the brakes hard and then fought to control the car's skid. They careened across the road, made a brief foray into the median, then slid all the way back into their original lane. Miraculously, nobody hit them in the course of this wild ride. The car came to rest at last on the edge of a steep embankment. In the sudden quiet, they watched as a hubcap cartwheeled down the hill, chrome glinting in the sun. They listened as the tire slowly deflated—sssssssss—and they felt the car settle with a bump over the flat.

Mrs. Entwhistle broke the silence. "Do you know how to change a tire, John?

~*~

This time she relented when John offered to drive the rest of the way back.

"I am about frazzled," she admitted. "I forgot how nerve-wracking it is to drive. I believe I'll just sit in the back seat, maybe close my eyes for a few minutes."

The sound of her snores soon filled the car. Maxine, too, put her head back and dozed. John squinted through the cracked windshield and drove gingerly on the spare tire. The ladies woke when he rolled gently to a stop at the dealership. Patting back their yawns, they disembarked, straightened their skirts, smoothed their hair and took a firm grip on their purses.

"John, did you fall? What are you doing down there? Are you kissing the ground?"

"No, ma'am, just tying my shoe."

"Well, I've been turning it over in my mind," Mrs. Entwhistle said, "and you know, I don't think I want to buy this car after all. I'd forgotten how exhausting driving can be. I usually just run errands in my neighborhood and my old Buick is fine for that. I believe I'll look into taking a remedial driving course. I know I can pass, and then Tommy will have to give my car back. I don't believe I should drive far, though."

"Why, honey, I'd be happy to take you anyplace you need to go," Maxine said. "I'll probably need to go myself. We'll make a day of it, have lunch and all. It'll be fun. I don't know why we didn't think of it before."

"And I'll buy our lunches," Mrs. Entwhistle said. She wanted to make sure Maxine knew she wasn't just sponging. She could pay her way.

"Well, that's settled then," she continued. "John, thank you kindly for the test ride."

Mrs. Entwhistle hated to see John looking so sad as he surveyed what was left of the new green Ford sedan. There was a long scratch on the driver's door, and the windshield was a web of cracks radiating from a central hole. The even smile of three fat chrome wheels was broken by the skinny black spare, and the back seat reeked of vomit. But really, she thought, a good clean-up with a little buffing would fix almost everything. Surely they were prepared for that at a dealership; it must happen all the time.

"I don't want you to get in trouble about the car getting a few dings and us being gone so long, and then not making a sale," she said. "'Cause you've been real nice."

"No, ma'am," he said. "Don't worry; I'll explain everything to Dad. Everything." He shivered a little.

"Tell your dad I said you're a credit to your raising. And you remember, John, you're a catch. You're a dream-boat."

"Yes, ma'am."

"Come on then, Max. Let's go home before it gets dark."

Mrs. Entwhistle Catches a Burglar

Roger's barking woke her. The old dog seldom bothered anymore. After almost fifteen years of life, there were few perils that Roger found worthy of the energy it took to bring forth his rusty *arf-arf*. Plus, barking made him sneeze. So when Roger delivered his midnight warning from the foot of her bed, Mrs. Entwhistle sat straight up, wide-awake in an instant.

"Roger, what is it? Hush, now, boy."

Snort, aaaah-choo.

Mrs. Entwhistle listened in the silence that followed Roger's explosive sneeze. Was that...? Yes, almost certainly, someone or something was moving around downstairs. She heard the floorboard in front of the corner cupboard creak, just as it did every time she stepped on it.

Nightingale floors, she thought; but this was not the time to review her Chinese history. Someone was in her house. She groped for her glasses on the bedside table and felt stronger when they were firmly on her nose. Moving carefully, she swung her legs over the side of the high bed and groped for her slippers. Grabbing her robe, she put it on and tied it around her waist.

18

Mrs. Entwhistle was not one to hide behind a locked bathroom door when someone was most likely stealing her money right out of the soup tureen in the corner cupboard. *That's my Social Security money*, she thought. The phone was beside her bed, but she didn't even glance at it as she reached for the thick cane she kept handy.

"Come on, Roger," she whispered. But Roger, feeling he'd done all that could reasonably be expected of him, had curled up in the warm spot she'd just vacated and regarded her drowsily. He wasn't going anywhere.

Mrs. Entwhistle moved quietly toward the stairway. Her late husband, a do-it-yourselfer, had installed dual switches at both the top and bottom of the steps, so lights could be turned on and off from either end. She crept down a few stairs in the dark and crouched to peer through the railings. She could see a dim rectangle where the French doors stood open, and a shadowy figure pawing through the contents of her cupboard. Mrs. Entwhistle felt a wash of anger. *Her* house, *her* stuff! Reaching back over her shoulder, she flipped the switch, flooding the room below with light. Running her cane along the banisters, she shouted, "Who are you? Get out of my house!"

The crouching figure shrieked and made for the open doors, but tripped on the ragged corner of an Oriental rug and sprawled headlong. Mrs. Entwhistle's daughter, Diane, had said just last weekend, "Mother, you are going to fall on that rug. You need to either get it mended or replaced. You really shouldn't have area rugs at all. They're just a tripping hazard."

Mrs. Entwhistle felt a fierce satisfaction that her

procrastination had paid off. "You!" she shouted. "Stay right where you are. The police are on the way."

Oops, I haven't called them yet. But he doesn't know that.

She went down the remaining stairs, remembering to hold carefully to the railing, and stood over the prone figure, cane aloft and ready to swing. But what was that? Crying? Did burglars cry when they got caught? For heaven's sake. She lowered her cane and prodded the body in the ribs.

"Sit up," she said, "and show me your hands." She felt proud of that particular piece of television dialog. It sounded authoritative, so she said it again. "Show me your hands! Don't try anything, or I'll whack you good."

"Don't hit me. Look, here are my hands. I'm sitting up now."

"Take that stupid ski cap off."

When the cap came off, a mane of blond hair fell down her captive's back.

"Why, Ronnie Sue Halpern!" Mrs. Entwhistle said, because it was her neighbor's teenage daughter. "Does your mother know you're here?"

"Please, please don't tell her," Ronnie Sue said, tears making tracks down her still-chubby cheeks.

"What…why…what are you doing?"

"I'm sorry, Mrs. Entwhistle, I'm so sorry. I just, I just needed some money in a hurry, and I remembered that you keep some extra cash in that soup thing. You got it out once to pay me when I was selling Girl Scout cookies, and I was going to pay it back just as soon as I could,

20

and…I'm really sorry."

"You need money so badly that you'd steal from *me*? *Your neighbor*?" Mrs. Entwhistle said.

"Could you – maybe - put your cane down?" Ronnie Sue said.

Mrs. Entwhistle realized she was still gripping it with white knuckles. She shook her head briskly, leaned the cane against the wall and eyed the girl at her feet. The child didn't look like she'd need to be walloped. In fact, she looked like she needed a tissue and a cup of tea, in that order. Mrs. Entwhistle produced these and sat Ronnie Sue down at her kitchen table.

"Now. Tell me about it."

"Well, see, my boyfriend - you've maybe noticed him when he comes to pick me up?"

"Is he that boy on the loud motorcycle?"

"Yes, ma'am. He tries to be quiet if it's real late, though."

"Well, he doesn't try hard enough. He's waked me and Roger several times. Tell him to get a muffler or something."

"Yes, ma'am, I will. I'll tell him. But, see, he—his name is Biff—"

Of course it is, Mrs. Entwhistle thought.

"—and Biff, well, I know you won't like this, but Biff has a little bit of a drug problem."

"There's no such thing as a little bit of a drug problem," Mrs. Entwhistle said.

Unpleasant memories surfaced of her son, Tommy, in his rebellious teenage years. Tommy had been what Mrs. Entwhistle learned to call a pothead. He simply loved to smoke dope and took every opportunity to do so, becoming less and less concerned when smoke drifted from under his bedroom door to stink up the whole house. His father'd had a fit. He'd taken his belt to Tommy. Yelled and grounded and restricted and withheld allowances. Mrs. Entwhistle had pleaded and bargained and shed tears. Nothing seemed to puncture Tommy's mellow mood and nothing stopped him from smoking all the marijuana he wanted.

He finally quit, but not before he was good and ready. Well, as far as she knew, he'd quit. Certainly the mellowness was gone; he'd become very bossy and judgmental of his mother's decisions. His wife recently packed up herself and the two kids and departed. Mrs. Entwhistle didn't know what precipitated that rupture. *Could it be that Tommy still…? Good grief, he's in his forties.* She jerked her mind back to the present and to the tear-stained girl before her.

"So…well, Biff owes some money to his - the guy he buys from. And that person is real mad that Biff can't pay him. He says he'll break Biff's legs if he doesn't pay by Tuesday, and…"

Ronnie Sue's halting narrative was drowned in another flood of tears. Mrs. Entwhistle handed her the whole tissue box. Eventually, her sobs abated, replaced with hiccups. She sounded like a baby who had eaten too fast. In spite of her outrage, Mrs. Entwhistle's heart softened. Ronnie Sue, at sixteen, really was still a baby, although a very naughty one. Clearly, she was in over her head. *If she was my daughter, she wouldn't be dating*

22

anyone yet, let alone someone like this Biff person.

"You've got to talk to your parents about this," she said.

"I can't. You know Mom has cancer, and the chemo makes her so sick, and Dad is trying to work and keep everything going at home. I can't give them any more problems."

"You should have thought of that before you broke into my house."

"Actually, I didn't break in. Your French doors weren't locked."

Mrs. Entwhistle digested that unwelcome bit of information. Diane had lectured about that too. "French doors aren't safe even when they are locked," she'd said, "and you forget to lock them half the time. All anyone would have to do is knock out a pane, reach in and turn the knob. You really need a burglar alarm, Mama."

But Mrs. Entwhistle was leery of those ticking time bombs that threatened to erupt if you weren't quick enough in entering your code. She'd seen Diane race to placate her alarm the minute she crossed her threshold. Who could remember a stupid number under such pressure? She'd have to write it down and tape it on the wall beside the alarm, which would certainly defeat the purpose. No, Roger would do just fine as a burglar alarm, and hadn't he proved it this very night?

As if summoned by her thoughts, Roger waddled stiffly down the stairs. His hind legs were lame and stairs were a trial for him, but he'd finally figured out that they had company and it was one of his favorite people, Ronnie Sue. He shuffled over to her and licked her legs.

"Eew, Roger, stop that!" she said.

The little dog plopped down at her feet and smiled up at her.

"You're a sweetie, aren't you, Roger? Who's a good boy? Who's a sweet, good doggums?" Ronnie Sue said in the falsetto voice that got Roger every time. He rolled over on his back, offering up his fat belly for rubbing.

"Never mind Roger right now," Mrs. Entwhistle said firmly, regaining control of the conversation. "I doubt that you want my advice, but since you broke into my home to steal from me, you're going to get it: let Biff solve his own problem. That's how we learn."

"But if he gets hurt!" Ronnie Sue's eyes were round with horror. "I'd never be able to live with myself if I let him get hurt."

"Ronnie Sue. Get a clue," Mrs. Entwhistle said, liking the rhyme as she heard it. "It's out of your control. This young man has issues. Don't make them your issues."

"But I lu-lu-love him," Ronnie Sue said, amid more floods of tears.

"Oh, for heaven's sake." Mrs. Entwhistle picked up her cane and thumped it on the floor. Ronnie Sue inhaled raggedly and mopped her tears.

"How much money does he need?" Mrs. Entwhistle asked.

"Four hundred dollars," Ronnie Sue said in a whisper.

Mrs. Entwhistle nodded. She thought for a minute.

Then she said, "All right then. Bring your young man to see me tomorrow."

~*~

Mrs. Entwhistle surprised herself by going back to sleep. When she awoke it was eight o'clock and the sun was streaming through her east bedroom window. Roger lay like a shaggy little bear in a nest he'd made in her robe. She tumbled him off unceremoniously. Eight o'clock! She couldn't remember when she'd slept so late. Heading to the kitchen for her first invigorating cup of tea, her eyes fell on the corner cupboard and the memory of her middle-of-the-night visitor floated up to the front of her mind.

What had she been thinking when she told Ronnie Sue to bring that gangster boy to see her? What did she know about drug addicts? Well, more than she ever wanted to know, but it's different when it's family. You can say anything to family and there's not much they can do about it. Besides, she knew very well that you can't talk anybody out of anything they really want to do. What if this Biff person decided to knock her down and take her money? Ronnie Sue may have told him where it was. Briefly, she thought about calling Diane and asking her advice, but the thought of the lecture that would follow made her feel she'd rather just be mugged and get it over with.

She went to the soup tureen and removed a pile of bills which she counted carefully, even though she knew how much was there: $830.13. Mrs. Entwhistle had been raised by depression-era parents; she could pinch pennies. With this money, she'd buy groceries and gas up her car, pay utilities, put some aside for the long-term care premium due next month, and maybe have enough left over for dinner and a movie with Maxine. Hmmm, maybe Max could come and keep her company her if Biff showed up. There'd be safety in numbers, even if it was just two little old ladies instead of one.

After eating a scrambled egg for protein, Mrs. Entwhistle set out to find Maxine. She knew that on Wednesday mornings, Maxine would be getting her hair done at the Curl-E-Cue Corner. She'd just go there and wait until Max was out from under the dryer and had a final comb-out and spray. They could talk over chicken salad.

~*~

The ladies snagged a desirable table in the Daily Diner, one that overlooked the town park so they could watch the kids on the playground. The diner, located in a former newspaper office, was decorated accordingly. Framed front pages going back forty years yellowed gently on the walls, and ancient manual typewriters squatted like metal gargoyles on the deep window ledges. On each table was a glass bowl containing printer's block letters, into which were stuck a few dusty artificial flowers. Their waitress, as ancient as the typewriters, made her way slowly to their table.

"Extra, extra," she said in a monotone, peering at them through her trifocals, "what can I get for you girls today?"

"Hi, Wanda," Mrs. Entwhistle said, "we'll have our usual."

No further explanation was necessary. Wanda nodded, not bothering to write anything on her pad, and crept toward the kitchen. In due time, two Ladies' Special

Chicken Salad Plates arrived at the same snail's pace.

"Well, Cora, what a pickle," Maxine said, having heard the whole story. She licked the final scrap of chicken salad off her fork. "My, weren't you brave, though, to go downstairs and catch that burglar!"

"It was only Ronnie Sue," Mrs. Entwhistle said.

"But you didn't know that. You could have gotten knocked over the head, or even shot." Maxine's eyes sparkled like the sequins on her glasses frames.

"Stop it, you sound just like Diane," Mrs. Entwhistle said. "I had my cane and I could have whacked anybody who tried to mess with me."

Maxine spoke carefully. "You know I don't mean to criticize, Cora. But sometimes we tend to forget how old we actually are now."

Maxine was being tactful. And really, there was some truth to what she said. Mrs. Entwhistle did tend to forget that she was an old woman. In her head, she felt about fifty. Her fifties had been a good time in her life. The kids were grown and gone, Floyd had still been alive and healthy and they had some extra time and money to spend on themselves. They'd had that one great trip through Canada on the train before Floyd got sick. If she could choose a time to go back to, she'd definitely choose the decade of her fifties.

"I expect you're right, Max. I admit I do feel uneasy about having that boy in my house while I'm there alone. Would you be a pal and come over and just be there with me when he comes?"

"Of course I will. My goodness, I should have thought to offer. Not that I'd be much help if things got rough."

"You could have your cell phone in your hand so he could see it, and he'd know that we could call for help in a second. Don't you think?"

"Yes, definitely. That's a good plan. I have 911 on speed dial. And I'll wear my police whistle around my neck. I could knock his ears off with one blast, I bet. What time do you expect him?"

"Well, I wouldn't think he'd come until after school's out this afternoon, so maybe right after three? Tell you what, why don't you just come on home with me now and we can work on my quilt until he gets there. I've got to finish the darn thing because Diane never will."

Mrs. Entwhistle's quilt was older than she was. Her mother had started but never finished it, and Mrs. Entwhistle inherited it. Every now and then when the spirit moved her, she unfolded it from its nest of blue tissue paper, enlisted Tommy's help in setting up the heavy wooden quilting frame and worked on it until her fingers bled. Then back into the tissue it would go. Maxine was always game to help, although her stitches were long and uneven. This was a secret grievance for Mrs. Entwhistle, but she reminded herself that beggars can't be choosers. Max meant well. And she did get a lot done by not worrying about making tiny, even stitches.

As they stitched quietly, Maxine cleared her throat and spoke. "Just what, exactly, are you going to say to this boy when he does come?"

"Why, I'll see what he's like. If he seems okay, but just young and stupid, I might offer him some work, let him earn money to pay off his drug debt so his legs won't get broken. I've got some things that need to be done."

"I see. What if he's mean?"

"If he is, I don't reckon he'll come."

But he did come, knocking on the door at three-twenty, with Ronnie Sue hanging on his arm.

"You wanted to see me, ma'am?" he asked politely enough.

"Ah yes, Ronnie Sue's young man. I am Mrs. Entwhistle. And you are…?"

"Oh, sorry, Mrs. Entwhistle. This is Biff," Ronnie Sue said, pride and love shining in her eyes.

Biff was not a prepossessing figure, in Mrs. Entwhistle's opinion. He was tall and of that extreme skinniness sometimes seen in teenage boys, the kind that makes you think you can see their beating hearts right through their bony chests. His long brown hair flopped over one eye, but it was shiny clean and he smelled of fabric softener. It was enough to make Mrs. Entwhistle conditionally forgive him for the bright red tattoo of a dragon on his forearm. She suspected it was the wash-off kind, anyway. She hoped so.

Mrs. Entwhistle glanced at Maxine, who sat holding her phone before her like a shield. Maxine nodded and lowered her phone. Mrs. Entwhistle stepped aside and motioned for the youngsters to enter.

Ronnie Sue had been in the house many times – most recently, the middle of last night – but Biff had to take a moment to look around him. Mrs. Entwhistle's house was furnished in a combination of hand-me-downs and pieces she and Floyd had saved up for over time.

29

Everything was still perfectly good (except for the frayed Oriental rug), so she saw no reason to change it. Biff's eyes shifted from the pink flowered sofa to the huge, chocolate brown recliner that had been Floyd's, to the delicate gate-leg table that came from Mrs. Entwhistle's mother, to the avocado green drapes. The corner cabinet, First Bank of Mrs. Entwhistle, stood by, still holding its tureen of cash.

"Wow," he said. "Like, wow. This is a real grandma house."

"I'll take that as a compliment," Mrs. Entwhistle said. "I understand you need money to pay your drug dealer." She didn't believe in beating around the bush.

Biff's eyes flew to Ronnie Sue. "You told her?"

"She caught me," Ronnie Sue said. "I had to tell her why I was…you know."

"In any case, I know all about it," Mrs. Entwhistle said. "I know about the $400 and the leg-breaking. Have you talked to your parents about this?"

Biff grimaced. "No point. Dad took off a couple years ago and Mom is either working or dating. She wouldn't want to be bothered."

"A school counselor? A minister? Family friend or relative?"

"No. They'd just send me to juvie for drugs."

"I see. Do you have an after-school job?"

"I'd like to have one. I've applied all over town, but I don't get hired."

"Humph," Mrs. Entwhistle said, thinking *no wonder.*

30

"What can you do?"

"I'm good at working on my motorbike, and I can cut grass and stuff. That's about it, but I can learn, and I'm a hard worker."

"I have some chores around here that need doing. I pay ten dollars an hour, but I expect you to give me a full hour's work for that money, and not be mooning around Ronnie Sue. I need the yard raked, the clothesline restretched, my car cleaned inside and out, this rug rolled up and carried to the repair shop, the kitchen cabinets wiped down, the hall bathroom painted, and windows washed."

Biff looked stunned, but game. "I can do all that, I think," he said. "I could come after school every day. When do you want me to start?"

"You can start today if you want to. But it's not going to solve your immediate leg-breaking problem. What are you going to do about that? You can probably make $400 working for me, but at $10 an hour, it will take you awhile. Do you think your...supplier...would be amenable to making a deal?"

"What kind of deal?"

"Tell him you'll give him one hundred dollars up front, and pay off the rest at one hundred dollars a month. Tell him it's better than nothing. And tell him you won't be purchasing any more of his products. Do you think he'll go for that?"

"Maybe. I don't have one hundred dollars, though."

Mrs. Entwhistle walked to her corner cabinet and took down the soup tureen. She removed the lid and showed Biff and Ronnie Sue the pile of bills inside,

31

ignoring Maxine's frantic head-shaking and phone-waving.

"This is where I keep my Social Security money," she said. "I need it to pay my bills. It's not extra; it's what I live on. I trust you not to steal it." She narrowed her eyes in the fierce Mom glare she'd perfected when her children were small. Both Biff and Ronnie Sue cowered before it. Good. If the glare still worked on these two, it meant they were not beyond hope.

She counted out five twenties and handed them to Biff. "Here. This is an advance on your first ten hours of work. Give it to your dealer."

She'd have to dip into her bank account to pay Biff the rest, if he actually did the work. Time would tell. The first chore was re-stretching the clothesline. Clearly, the boy had never seen one before.

"Is this some kind of old-time dryer?" he asked, eyeing the green plastic line sagging between two cross-shaped poles.

"This is a clothes line," Mrs. Entwhistle said. "I hang my washing on it when the weather is good. Then I don't have to use the dryer, which saves money on electricity, and the clothes smell like fresh air."

"Huh," Biff said.

"Now, unknot the line here at this end…that's right…now pull. Pull! And retie it tight. Very good. See how much better that is? Now my sheets won't drag on the ground."

Biff seemed heartened by his successful completion of the first chore. Mrs. Entwhistle thought briefly of Hercules cleaning the Augean Stables, or Sisyphus continuously pushing that rock up the hill.

Training this boy might be like that, for both of them. They soldiered on. She found he needed step-by-step instructions on performing the simplest tasks. That he'd never been taught to do anything around the house was painfully apparent. Mrs. Entwhistle stayed on him, and to his credit, he never complained or asked for a break. She liked that.

Two hours later, Biff had raked the yard, pulled weeds along the back fence and swept out the garage. He had a smudge of dirt under his nose and his arms were scratched. He looked exhausted.

"You've just paid me back $20," Mrs. Entwhistle said. "Are you going to come again? Or have I thrown my money away?"

"I'll come back tomorrow," Biff said, lifting his chin in what Mrs. Entwhistle thought was a commendable show of spirit.

"All right, then. See that you do."

With no further ceremony, she went into the house and shut the door. Mrs. Entwhistle was not given to praise, and surely effusive thanks were uncalled for under the circumstances. Her legs felt like logs from so much standing and a niggling little headache was tormenting her left eye. Following a good smell to her kitchen, she found Maxine stirring a pot of homemade potato soup.

"Come on, Cora, sit down. I've made us some soup. You'll feel better after you eat."

~*~

Biff showed up the next day with a black eye.

"What happened? Who hit you?" Mrs. Entwhistle

asked.

"My dealer wanted to make sure I understood he wasn't happy about having to wait for the rest of his money."

"Did you give him the hundred?"

"Yes. He took it. Then he punched me."

"Well, at least your legs still work. Could be worse." Mrs. Entwhistle was not sympathetic about predictable consequences. "Better get to work."

And work he did. Biff made up his hundred dollar advance in five days. On Saturday, he worked eight hours and Mrs. Entwhistle had to drive to the ATM and get eighty dollars in cash to pay him.

"Now, make sure you don't spend this on a date with Ronnie Sue or worse yet, on more dope," she said as she handed him the little envelope.

"No, ma'am, Ronnie Sue is behind me one hundred per cent," Biff said. "She won't let me spend a penny. Once I get this debt paid, I hope I never see another bag of weed again in my life. It's not worth it."

Biff was dependable, arriving on his noisy motorcycle every day as soon as school was out. Mrs. Entwhistle wondered when he did his homework, if he did it at all. But that was not her concern. She wasn't interested in mothering Biff. As long as he did his chores reasonably well in a reasonable amount of time, she was content. It was a business deal. If she occasionally wondered at herself for getting involved with a couple of juvenile delinquents, she reasoned that neighbors help neighbors, and Ronnie Sue's family needed it right now. Heading off trouble was Mrs. Entwhistle's little bit of help.

And really, things did seem to be working out well. Biff only had a few more hours and he'd have enough to pay the last installment to his drug dealer.

~*~

Mrs. Entwhistle and Maxine decided to take in a matinee. "That new movie…you know," she said, "with that young man with the beautiful blue eyes…we saw him in that other movie with the little blonde girl…remember?"

"Oh, I know who you mean. Yes, I want to see that one, too," Maxine said.

Old peoples' shorthand, Mrs. Entwhistle called it. But they understood each other perfectly, and so on a sunny Tuesday afternoon they arrived at the Cineplex at one-thirty for the first show. Maxine drove her enormous Lincoln Navigator, peering just over the rim of the steering wheel. She'd wanted a tall vehicle so she could see all around, she'd said, but it hadn't exactly worked out that way. Sitting on cushions to give her a boost helped a little, but the cushions had an unsettling tendency to slip out from under her when she braked.

"It looks more dangerous than it actually is," she said. Mrs. Entwhistle nodded agreeably. If Max could keep that enormous contraption in her lane, how she did it was her business.

Two hours and a giant, shared bucket of popcorn later, the ladies chatted happily as they returned home through the light mid-afternoon traffic. Maxine slipped neatly into Mrs. Entwhistle's driveway with the ease of much practice.

"Why don't you come in for a cup of tea, Max?" Mrs. Entwhistle said. "I need something to wash away all that buttered popcorn."

"Me, too. Wasn't it good, though?"

The first surprise was seeing that the kitchen door was slightly open. The second being met at the threshold by Roger, since he was usually deeply asleep on a sofa pillow at this time of day. His filmy old eyes were wide and terrified in a strangely white face.

"Why, Roger! What's the matter, boy?"

Looking around, Mrs. Entwhistle answered her own question: everything. The contents of her kitchen were strewn on the floor. A flour bag had been ripped open and a layer of white coated all surfaces, including Roger. Sugar and salt gritted underfoot as she hurried to the archway between the kitchen and dining room. Sure enough, the soup tureen lay in pieces amid the wreckage of her corner cupboard.

Before Mrs. Entwhistle could find words, the familiar roar of Biff's motorbike filled the air. She caught a glimpse of movement out of the corner of her eye. Maxine screamed and let loose ear-splitting blasts on her police whistle. With a snarl, Roger launched himself across the room at a most uncharacteristic speed. Mrs. Entwhistle whirled, struggled for balance, raised her cane high and brought it down with all her strength across the back of a young man bent double, trying to dislodge Roger from his leg. Biff hit the door at a dead run and joined Roger's attack, accompanied by more screams from Ronnie Sue.

"Stop! Get off me, get this damn dog off, stop hitting!" the intruder yelled into the din. "Here, take the friggin' money. Just let me out of here."

Twenties fluttered to the floor and Roger and Biff

were flung away as the intruder made a frantic dash for freedom. The last glimpse they had of him was his retreating back and pumping legs.

"Did you know him, Biff?" Mrs. Entwhistle spoke at last into the blessed silence.

"He's—he was—my dealer," Biff said. "He must have followed me here one day. He knew I was getting money from an after-school job to pay him. I'm sorry, Mrs. Entwhistle. I brought him down on you."

"Never mind, Biff," Mrs. Entwhistle said, "We fixed him, didn't we? I knew this cane would come in handy someday. It's better than Mace. And Roger! What a good dog, Rog."

Maxine wielded the broom and dustpan, and Ronnie Sue picked up shards of broken dishes and put them in a trash bag. Biff took Roger outside and brushed the flour from his coat, after which the old dog lapped up a sizeable amount of water and subsided with a groan on his favorite pillow. With all of them working together, the house returned to normal in a surprisingly short time. Mrs. Entwhistle looked at the clock.

"Good gracious. Here it is, almost six o'clock and I haven't even thought about supper. Are y'all hungry?"

"I'll get us a pizza," Biff said.

"Here, let me…" Mrs. Entwhistle looked around for her purse.

"No, ma'am. It's my treat."

Mrs. Entwhistle smiled. "All right then."

It was her money, after all.

Mrs. Entwhistle Delivers Meals-on-Wheels

"Mother, you simply can't do it. You're old enough to get meals delivered to you, not deliver them to other people."

Diane looked indignant, concerned and solicitous. Like a mother. Like Mrs. Entwhistle's mother. Oh no, this would not do.

"Diane, I'm perfectly able to make my own decisions," Mrs. Entwhistle said. "If I choose to fill in for a couple of days while the regular delivery person has a root canal, then that's what I'll do."

"But some of the people probably live in upstairs apartments without elevators. Do you think you can carry those heavy food packages upstairs?"

"Certainly," Mrs. Entwhistle said. "I carried you and Tommy up enough stairs, and you weighed more than food packages."

"Yes, but that was forty years ago. Be realistic, Mother. You're not..."

Mrs. Entwhistle fixed Diane with her most ferocious glare. It worked when Diane was a child and it worked now. She subsided, although she looked like she had plenty more to say. Mrs. Entwhistle did not want to hear it. I'm being mothered by my own daughter, she thought. As if she suddenly became so wise and almighty, and I became the child. Mrs. Entwhistle was determined now to deliver those meals if she had to crawl on her hands and knees, carrying them in her teeth.

Maxine had given up her volunteer job as a meal deliverer a few years back, but she still worked one day a week answering phones. It was she who mentioned to Mrs. Entwhistle that they were looking for a temp to fill in for a regular carrier who was having dental surgery.

"I'd do it myself," Max said, "but it's hard to get in and out of the car so many times." Maxine had a bad hip.

"I'll do it," Mrs. Entwhistle said.

"Cora, I don't think—they probably would want someone young…" Maxine stopped short. Talk of aging was like waving a red flag before Mrs. Entwhistle's bull-headedness.

~*~

The Meals on Wheels director, Gloria Lomax, was desperate. Losing one volunteer for a couple of days wouldn't ordinarily be such a big deal, but the roster was especially slim right now.

"And I've got to go to Chicago to help my daughter. She's having her first baby, and I want to see her through the first week at home."

"Of course you should go," Mrs. Entwhistle said.

"The first baby is a huge deal. All the showers and doctor visits and packing your little overnight bag and getting the nursery ready. And once the baby comes, everybody wants to visit and you're so tired all you want to do is sleep. After you have the second, you might get a couple of cards. Go for the third, and people will say, 'Oh, did you have another one?' Your daughter needs you. She won't forgive you if you miss this."

Mrs. Entwhistle knew whereof she spoke. Diane had required her mother's presence when little Jeannie was born. There were mountains of disposable diapers (of which Mrs. Entwhistle did not approve) and sore nipples and misunderstandings and tears. It had not been an easy time, but she'd understood the necessity of being there for her daughter. When Diane had Junior three years later, it was a different story. She'd simply hung him in a sling around her neck and gotten on with her life. Mrs. Entwhistle actually missed the new-baby drama the second time around. Being part of it had made her feel needed and useful – a real mother again. She jerked her thoughts back to the moment.

"But – I don't know if you – I mean, it's fairly strenuous," Gloria's voice trailed off uncertainly. "Well, what the heck. Why don't you try it, and if it's too much…" her voice dried up, caught in the hot light of Mrs. Entwhistle's glare.

A little opposition, a hint of you-can't-do-it, was like a double-dog-dare to Mrs. Entwhistle, and nothing would have kept her from showing up for duty on the appointed day. The warehouse-like room was brightly lighted and filled with people in hairnets packing little white boxes, sealing them up and passing them along to the loading table. A large man effortlessly stacked six boxes in his arms and deposited them in Mrs. Entwhistle's car trunk.

"There you go, honey," he said, with a pat on Mrs. Entwhistle's arm. "Here's a city map with your route highlighted. Think you can find the addresses? Know how to read the map?"

"Of course," Mrs. Entwhistle said frostily. Honestly, why did everyone just automatically assume she couldn't function? Actually, she couldn't read a map – never could, but she wouldn't admit it for anything. Anyway, she had an ace in the hole: an after-market navigation system that her son, Tommy, had given her for Christmas.

"It's real easy, Mama," he'd said. "You just put in the address and press Go and a voice will give you street by street directions. Here, do you want me to program in the voice with a British accent?"

"Sure. Every word spoken with a British accent sounds intelligent," Mrs. Entwhistle said. She named the voice Queen Elizabeth. Queenie had already steered her dependably around the neighborhood in trial runs, and Mrs. Entwhistle was eager to take their relationship on the road for a real test. She laboriously entered the first address. It was for J. Cameron.

"Please drive the highlighted route," Queenie said crisply. Mrs. Entwhistle put the car in gear and she was off. Thankfully, Queenie did more than display a map; she also spoke and gave accurate directions to the first destination, a little Craftsman cottage that had seen better days. Carrying a white box in one hand and her cane in the other, Mrs. Entwhistle stepped with care up the uneven flagstone walk. She rang the bell, but hearing no inner peal, knocked as well. There was a long pause during which nothing happened, so she knocked again a little harder. Finally, she heard a shuffling, sliding sound on the other side of the door.

"Keep your damn pants on," a voice snarled. The door opened an inch and an eye appeared in the crack. "What do you want?"

"Meals on Wheels," Mrs. Entwhistle said, thinking this recipient might soon be wearing his dinner.

"Oh. C'mon in, then."

The owner of the eye backed up and opened the door wider. As Mrs. Entwhistle stepped inside, she saw that her client was leaning heavily on a walker.

"That's not the way you're supposed to use a walker," she said. "You're supposed to stand up straight, not lean forward like that. My late husband, Floyd, had to go to rehab to learn how to use his walker correctly."

"Well, bully for Floyd. What'd you bring me to eat?"

"I think it's some kind of chicken, salad, green beans..."

But the man didn't wait to hear the whole menu. With a grunt, he took the white box out of Mrs. Entwhistle's hand, balanced it on the seat of his walker and headed off toward what she presumed was the kitchen. "Let yourself out," he said.

"You're welcome," Mrs. Entwhistle said, and gave the door a bang behind her.

Queenie had a harder time finding the next address and Mrs. Entwhistle had to circle the block. "Shape up, Queenie," she muttered, finally finding a parking place in the deck beside the high-rise senior apartment building. She took the elevator up to the fifth floor and knocked on

5D, the home of one T. Muir. The door flew open while her hand was still raised. Before her stood a tiny woman dressed entirely in pink.

"Oh, are you with Meals on Wheels?" The woman had the tinkly, high-pitched voice of a five year old. "Come in, come in. I'm so glad to see you. What's the weather like out there? I don't get out much anymore, now that I'm living in this apartment. I used to have a house, you know, and a beautiful yard. I grew roses, my favorites were the pink tea roses, but oh my, they got so many bugs and black spots, I was just constantly spraying them. My neighbors used to say, Thelma, you'll poison us all with that insecticide, but of course they were just kidding. Mr. Gramercy that lived across the street, I think he was a little bit sweet on me, but he was too shy to say anything. And what would I want with a sick old man? That's what they're after, you know, when they get past sex: they want a woman to take care of them. Well, not me; I did my share of that, and –."

Mrs. Entwhistle cut across the relentless patter of words, her naturally loud voice rising to be heard. "Here's your dinner. Where do you want it?"

"Why, right here on the table. My, doesn't that look good! You are so kind to bring it. I used to do volunteer work; I was a Pink Lady at the hospital. Well, you could say I'm still a pink lady—"

"Eat it while it's hot. Goodbye."

Mrs. Entwhistle's ears were ringing as she made her way down the elevator, into her car, through the deck and back onto the street. After only two stops, she was already feeling a little winded. Well, one thing for sure, Diane would never know that.

The next client, R. Blanding, was a little old lady who eyed the food box with frightening intensity.

"Have you eaten today?" Mrs. Entwhistle asked.

"No, this will be my first meal," came the reply, "and the last. One meal a day is plenty for old folks, don't you think?"

Mrs. Entwhistle thought of her own breakfast this morning: thick, creamy oatmeal, a slice of heavily buttered toast and a little pot of Earl Grey. She thought of the two meals still to come, both of which would be ample because she believed in eating well. Then she decided to let it pass, to allow the woman to make her own decisions about intake. Food was one of the last bastions of autonomy for the very old.

A couple, listed as E. and M. Gray, answered the door in tandem at her next stop. Her mind flashed the thought Tweedledee and Tweedledum, for they were as round as butterballs and wore matching red tracksuits.

"Come on in, sugar," the man said.

"Yes, we've been expecting you…oh, you're not our regular, are you?" the woman said, peering at Mrs. Entwhistle. Her inch-deep spectacles made her eyes look huge. "You're most welcome, anyway," she continued. "Would you like to sit down and eat with us? We'll share, there's always plenty. We do so love to have company."

Mrs. Entwhistle explained that she hadn't finished her rounds yet and weathered the disappointment in the friendly couple's eyes. Making her way to her next stop, she wondered if the Tweedles had children to check on them and provide some company. Even bossy children like her own were better than none. Sometimes food just wasn't enough to fill the emptiness.

Queenie directed her next to a tumble-down little house crouched at the curb in a neighborhood that made the hairs stand up on the back of her neck. Hurrying as fast as she could, she knocked on the sagging front door, hoping to get in and out before the muggers spotted her.

She knocked again and heard a faint voice call, "Come in, please." The door opened with a push. The room within was stifling and so dark that Mrs. Entwhistle's eyes had to take a minute to adjust before they could make out the shadowy figure lying on an ancient sofa.

"Wheels on, I mean, Meals on Wheels," she said, feeling flustered by the claustrophobic atmosphere.

"Yes. Come over here, would you? I can't get up today."

The stench of a thousand unchanged cat boxes made Mrs. Entwhistle's stomach lurch as she approached the reclining figure, unsure if she was looking at a man or a woman. She took in stringy, greasy gray hair, and a dingy T-shirt stretched over unmistakable breasts – yes, it was a woman. Several felines reposed on the backs of chairs and on tables. They regarded Mrs. Entwhistle unblinkingly. Cat hair drifted like tumble-weeds on the floor. It clung to the walls and upholstery. One of the cats sneezed, spraying out a fine mist of cat snot.

"Aren't you the nicest thing, to bring me a good meal!" the woman said, comfortable in her fur-lined world. "I'm Angelina. Isn't it funny that I share a name with that beautiful movie star? My mother was Cajun, that's where my name came from. I'm just fortunate it's not Evangeline, right?"

Angelina's laugh ended in a rattling cough as she struggled to sit upright. "If you'd just push that little table over here...that's right...and put the food on it. Good, that's all I need. It smells delicious. Thank you so much."

"Um – Angelina – do you need more help than a meal?" Mrs. Entwhistle asked bluntly.

"What do you mean?"

"Well, you know, maybe some assistance with housework or personal care."

"Oh, no, I'm fine. I'm perfectly fine just the way I am. You're nice to ask, though."

"Do you have any relatives that look in on you, or do you have home health care?"

"I sure do. And they all want to clean the house and scrub me up one side and down the other. I appreciate it, I do, but I'm fine, really. No point in getting all gussied up just to stay at home."

Mrs. Entwhistle fetched a glass of tap water from the disgusting kitchen, deposited it on Angelina's table, said her goodbyes and went on her way.

"Whatever works," she said aloud. "Who am I to judge? You'd think she'd be itchy, though, in all that cat hair."

A passer-by looked at her curiously. Sometimes she forgot and talked to herself in public, drawing stares and sometimes laughter. Well, big deal. People can just get over it.

That night, Mrs. Entwhistle stretched out on her bed with a groan she was glad Diane couldn't hear. Okay, maybe it was a bit too much, all that getting in and out of the car, all the walking and carrying. Still, she'd do it again the next day because she'd said she would. Roger, her ancient Shih'tsu, settled comfortably on the pillow beside her head. For fifty-some years, Mrs. Entwhistle had awakened to the sight of Floyd's whiskery face; now it was Roger's.

Before she went to sleep, her mind replayed the day and the people she'd met. They all shared one common denominator: loneliness. She imagined them crouched over the little food boxes, alone in their homes. By morning, an idea had sprouted fully formed in her head.

The route was easier the next day. She knew the territory now, knew what to expect. She banged loudly on the cranky man's door and waited while he shuffled to answer it.

"Here's your food," she said, when his baleful eye appeared in the crack of the door.

"Yeah, well, don't just stand there, bring it on in," he said, but he left her to push the door open.

"Do you ever get out?" she asked him.

"None of your damn business," he said.

"Looks like you could get yourself out of this house a little bit. There are people out there worse off than you. You could maybe help somebody else instead of being such a danged old crab."

"Thank you, Mother Teresa," he said.

"I'm going to come back for you when I finish my deliveries," she said. "My name is Cora Entwhistle. What's yours?"

"Not that it's any of your beeswax, but my name is James Cameron. My friends call me J.C. You can call me Mr. Cameron."

"Well, Mr. Cameron, be ready at two o'clock. And I mean dressed, shaved, combed and ready to get out of here. I'll be back."

Mrs. Entwhistle exited quickly before he could say no, again giving the door a satisfying bang.

She continued on her route, taking care to learn first names as she went. The hungry lady's full name was Ramona Blanding. The friendly couple consisted of Myrna and Exeter Gray. Exeter? Well, no one could help what their mamas named them. The cat woman was Angelina Latrec. Pink Lady was Thelma Muir. Mrs. Entwhistle delivered their meals and told them to be ready around two because she'd be back. They all had excuses why it wouldn't be possible for them to get out that day; they looked scared and excited at the same time. Mrs. Entwhistle paid them no mind. She repeated her instruction: be ready at two. She'd nearly finished her route before it dawned on her that she couldn't get six more people in her car, even thought it was a big old Buick. She called Maxine.

"Max, I need your help," she began. "I want to haul some folks – six, to be exact – and it just occurred to me that I can't get that many in my car. Do you suppose you'd have time to help me this afternoon?" She outlined her plan.

"Why, sure," Maxine said. "Tell me where and when."

She assigned Maxine the Grays, and Ramona.

"Just tell them you're my friend and you're picking them up to help me out," Mrs. Entwhistle said.

Mr. Cameron, Angelina and Thelma she'd transport herself. As good natured as Maxine was, she couldn't ask her to put up with a smelly lady, a crabby man and a pink non-stop talker.

At two o'clock, she knocked on Mr. Cameron's door, fearing there would be no answer. But the door was opened almost immediately, as if he'd been standing there waiting for her. He had shaved and smelled strongly of cologne. Good, it may drown out some of Angelina's odor, Mrs. Entwhistle thought. She noticed that he had on a shirt that still contained the creases from the packaging. He'd obviously gone to some trouble to be presentable.

"Come on, let's get going, wherever the hell we're going," he muttered as he bumped his walker down the uneven walk to her car. She helped him into the front seat, folded his walker and stowed it in the trunk with some difficulty.

"Lock the doors," she instructed him as she pulled to the curb in front of Angelina's house. The neighborhood hadn't improved overnight. There was a small gaggle of teenagers at the corner, yelling and pushing each other around. They fell silent and stared ominously as Mrs. Entwhistle took a firm grip on her cane, straightened her spine and made her way to Angelina's door. Again, it swung open before she'd knocked twice.

"Hi, dearie," Angelina said, but Mrs. Entwhistle was too taken aback to reply. Angelina had transformed herself. Scrubbed pink, her clean hair pulled back with a colorful headband, wearing faded but spotless clothing of another era, Angelina looked nothing like the slovenly figure of yesterday. The odor wafting out her front door suggested that the only transformation had been to her person, but Mrs. Entwhistle was glad to settle for that.

Together, the two elderly ladies made their way to the car, inspiring another round of silent staring from the teenagers.

"Hi, Pablo, hi, Curtis, hi, Jerry Lee. Tell your mamas I said hi," Angelina called out to them. There was a nervous shuffling of feet at the mention of mamas, and the atmosphere of menace relaxed.

"Why, they're just children," Mrs. Entwhistle said.

"Of course. And I've known them since they were babies," Angelina said. "They're trying to figure out what to do with themselves now. Not much opportunity around here."

Mrs. Entwhistle helped her into the back seat and introduced her to James Cameron, who vouchsafed only a grunt of acknowledgement.

One more stop, to pick up Thelma, and all need for conversation ceased. Everyone relaxed, letting the tide of Thelma's monologue wash over them. No replies were expected, or even possible. It was oddly restful.

They saw Maxine when they arrived, cheerfully assisting Ramona, Myrna and Exeter out of her Lincoln Navigator. She'd taken up two parking spaces, but it was hard to park a vehicle that big.

Introductions were made again, and the little party entered the Westside Senior Center. The smell of baking cookies greeted them in the common room. Mrs. Entwhistle pushed two tables together, seated everyone and brought them cups of coffee. Any awkwardness soon melted away, warmed by Maxine's conversational expertise. Skillfully, she asked just the right questions, got everyone talking and even convinced Thelma to take a breath. Maxine always was a great hostess, Mrs. Entwhistle thought gratefully. She knew she'd taken a big risk, gathering this group of strangers together.

Exeter spotted a deck of cards. "Does anyone like to play bridge?" he asked hopefully. "Myrna and I love to play, but just for fun. We're not cutthroat or anything."

Mr. Cameron looked up, his eyes alight. "Yeah, I play," he said. "Haven't played in years, but I think I still remember how."

Angelina smiled shyly. "I used to play. I wasn't very good, but I enjoyed it. If you promise to be patient with me while I remember the rules, I'll try it."

Ramona and Thelma wandered over to watch a table of beaders at work. Invited to join in, they were provided with needles, fishing line, a basket of beads and instructions. Even Thelma was silenced as their heads bent in concentration. Mrs. Entwhistle noticed that Ramona had stuffed cookies into her pockets for later.

The card table was equally focused, and Mrs. Entwhistle caught snatches of their conversation. "No, you can't bid no-trump with only ten points." "Oops, I reneged. I should have played that spade last hand." "Mr. Cameron, will you look at my hand now that you're the dummy?" "You can all call me J.C."

"Huh. I hauled his sorry backside in here, but *they* can call him J.C.," Mrs. Entwhistle whispered to Max.

Maxine laughed and made a circle with her thumb and finger. Mrs. Entwhistle nodded. Today, and maybe just for today, six lonely people were being nourished in ways that had nothing to do with food.

"I'll see how it goes," she said to Maxine. "Maybe we'll do this again."

Mrs. Entwhistle Enters

the Witness Protection Program

Hanging out her sheets on a sweet, breezy May morning, Mrs. Entwhistle thought with satisfaction that when she climbed into her bed that night, it would smell of springtime. Why would anyone use a dryer on such a day, she wondered, as the crisp cotton pillow cases snapped in the breeze.

Turning to retrieve her cane from where it hung on the clothesline's crossbar, she saw a strange car turn into her driveway. It stopped and disgorged two extremely official-looking personages. They wore matching navy blue windbreakers with such large letters printed on the back that she could read them from across the yard: USMS.

"Swanee," Mrs. Entwhistle said aloud, "What now?"

The strangers' appearance telegraphed law enforcement. She immediately felt guilty, although she couldn't think of anything she'd done wrong.

"Good morning," she called, wielding her cane carefully as she approached them over the rough spring grass. "Can I help you?"

"Cora Entwhistle?" the male member of the team said, looking down at the papers in his hand.

"Yes, I'm Cora Entwhistle," she replied. "And you are?"

"Deputy Marshal McClellen and Deputy Marshal Seeger of the United States Marshal Service, ma'am," he said, flipping open a leather case to reveal a large gold shield. "We're here to take you to your safe house."

"Take me to what?"

"We've got orders to take you into protective custody. You're in danger, ma'am. Marshal Seeger will help you get your things together, and then we've got to get you out of here. Right now."

"But why? What danger? What about Roger? I can't go anywhere without Roger."

"Roger? We weren't informed of any Roger."

On cue, Roger waddled around the corner of house, gave a desultory bark or two and then sneezed so violently that he had to lie down. Roger didn't get excited about much of anything anymore. He trusted Mrs. Entwhistle to handle whatever needed handling.

"That's Roger, right there," Mrs. Entwhistle said, "and he goes where I go. But why do I have to go anywhere?"

"Ma'am, I can't stress strongly enough the danger of your position. Our orders are to see to it that you stay safe," Marshal McClellen said, fixing her with a steely eye that brooked no nonsense.

Despite her innate contrariness, Mrs. Entwhistle felt a shiver of fear, a ground-fog of confusion and a strong sense that she'd better obey. She didn't know what they were talking about, but these poker-faced strangers oozed authority and if there was one thing she'd been taught in her youth, it was to respect authority.

"I better call Maxine and ask her to water my plants," she said, eyeing the newly-planted window boxes.

"You will call no one," Marshal McClellen said. "We'll see to your plants."

Trying for moral outrage, Mrs. Entwhistle thumped her cane on the ground. "Well, for goodness sake," she said, but her voice sounded weak and uncertain to her own ears.

Marshal Seeger, the female half of the team, took Mrs. Entwhistle's arm and steered her firmly toward the house. "Let's get you packed, ma'am. The sooner we can get going, the better," she said.

~*~

Later, Mrs. Entwhistle wondered why she'd submitted so meekly to those bossy strangers. Yes, their badges looked official, but you could probably buy them on the Ultranet, or whatever it was. After a long car ride in which Mrs. Entwhistle had to sit in the back seat behind darkly-tinted windows and all her conversational gambits were met with stony silence, they stopped at a nondescript white frame house on an ordinary suburban street.

"This looks a lot like my street, actually," Mrs.

Entwhistle said. The agents did not respond. "Roger probably needs to go out. He's old, he can't wait forever."

"Stay in the car," Deputy Marshal Seeger said. And again, Mrs. Entwhistle did as she was told. She watched the two marshals walk up the path, unlock the door and disappear inside. In five minutes, they were back, opening the car door, motioning for her to get out.

Roger, clipped to his leash, tugged Mrs. Entwhistle to a patch of thin grass, lifted his leg, lost his balance and settled for a squat. It took him a long time to empty his bladder, and when this was accomplished, he blinked up at her, waiting for whatever happened next. She knew how he felt.

Marshals Seeger and McClellan escorted her into the house. The front door opened directly into a living room furnished with a cheap, imitation leather sectional and a wood-veneer coffee table set against a wall, holding a television set. That was all. The kitchen was equally bare. Mrs. Entwhistle looked around curiously, wondering what all this had to do with her.

"Your bedroom is back here, ma'am," Marshal Seeger said, pointing down a narrow hallway.

"My bedroom?" Mrs. Entwhistle said. "No, you are mistaken. I've never been in this house before. I'm ready to go home now."

"This is home for a while, ma'am. You'll be staying here until the trial. There will be a guard posted twenty-four hours a day until then. You'll be perfectly safe as long as no one knows you're here. We strongly caution you to stay inside. We will provide you with a phone, but it will only take incoming calls."

"But what about my children? They'll be worried if they can't get me on the phone."

"We've arranged for your calls to be forwarded from your home line. Just don't say where you are when you talk to them. Are they apt to visit?"

"Well…no, not really. We just got together for Diane's birthday last week, so it will be a while before they come by again. They're so busy, you see, and I don't need their help." She lifted her chin slightly and stared Marshal Seeger in the eye. Nobody was going to get away with the slightest implication that Diane and Tommy were not the most solicitous of children.

"But what I'd like to know is why I'm here," Mrs. Entwhistle continued. "I don't know anything about a trial. I just want to go home."

"Very convincing," Marshal McClellan said. "You've been well-prepped. You keep that up. There's food in the pantry and an agent in a car at the curb if you need anything."

"I need to go home," she said, but the agents were already out the door.

~*~

Mrs. Entwhistle was flummoxed. "Roger, what the heck just happened?" she asked. Roger, as was his custom, did not reply. She walked through the house, which consisted of living room, kitchen, bathroom, and two small bedrooms, one of which was unfurnished. It took about two minutes. She stepped out onto the miniscule front porch. At the curb, in a nondescript sedan, sat a young man.

57

"Yoo-hoo!" Mrs. Entwhistle called. "You out there in the car. Could you come here for a minute?"

The young man hastily exited the car, looking over both shoulders. "Shhhh, ma'am, we don't want to call attention to ourselves," he whispered as he approached.

Mrs. Entwhistle heard only isolated words of this communication. "What?" she asked in her normal tone of voice, which was loud. "I'm sorry, honey, I didn't catch all that."

By now they were at the door and the young man bundled her inside with a firm hand between her shoulder blades. Mrs. Entwhistle mustered her dignity.

"Young man – what is your name, anyway?"

"Deputy Marshal Peters, ma'am."

"Do you have a first name?"

"Yes, ma'am, it's Pete."

"Pete Peters? Peter Peters?"

"Yes, ma'am."

"Well, you poor child. Anyway – Pete. I wanted to ask you - and I hope you'll be more informative than your colleagues - what am I doing here? Have I been kidnapped?"

"You're in protective custody until you testify at the trial, ma'am, you know that."

"I don't know that. What trial? I don't know anything about a trial or testimony or anything. Those two just came and got me – oh, dear, I left my sheets on the clothesline; they didn't give me time to think. Now here I am, and I don't know why."

Pete frowned. "I'm really not at liberty to discuss this with you, ma'am. I'm just supposed to make sure you're safe. I'd better get back out to the car now." And he was gone.

Roger was looking uneasy, and she thought he probably needed to go out again. She opened the back door, and they stepped into a tidy but totally uninspired space enclosed by a chain link fence. Roger walked straight to the fence, tail wagging, and greeted a very small human clinging to the other side. *Arf*, he said, meaning, "Here's something interesting. Look, Mom."

Mrs. Entwhistle looked. The child seemed to be no more than two. He or she wore only a diaper, and it was hanging low. Huge brown eyes surrounded by thick lashes peered at her over a thoroughly sucked thumb. She walked over and knelt down, ignoring the protests of her knees.

"Hello, there," she said.

No response. Roger licked the little hands and elicited a squeal. "Doggie, doggie!" the child said.

"His name is Roger. Do you want to pet him?"

A tiny hand reached through the chain link and batted at Roger's nose. He looked delighted at this turn of events, even though he didn't like to have his face touched. Apparently Roger was a pushover for babies. Who knew? There hadn't been any babies in Mrs. Entwhistle's life since her grandchildren outgrew that stage when Roger was just a pup.

Mrs. Entwhistle looked toward the house next door, hoping to spot the child's mother. That diaper really did need attention. But the house was quiet and shuttered, with no sign of life stirring within or without.

"Where's your mama?" she asked, but the toddler was engrossed with Roger and didn't even glance her way.

"Pete!" she called. Mrs. Entwhistle had a naturally carrying voice. She didn't mean to roar, but often she did without realizing it. "Pete!"

Marshal Peters scurried around the house. "Please, ma'am, keep your voice down."

"Pete, look here at this baby out in the yard all alone. What do you make of that? I'm going next door to get its mama. You watch Roger and the baby."

"No, I can't—you can't--"

But Mrs. Entwhistle was gone, plying her cane rapidly over the ground, then using it as a knocker. Repeated thumps brought no response. Meanwhile, the baby's diaper had given up its fight with gravity and was now adorning the grass.

"Well, at least we know it's a boy," Mrs. Entwhistle said. "We can't let him run around naked." She pronounced it nekkid. "Pete, you'll have to go to the store for diapers."

Pete began to protest when the little figure at their feet suddenly turned into a fountain.

"Just go on, now," Mrs. Entwhistle said. "You could get in trouble for child neglect."

Although this was clearly illogical, Pete retreated rapidly to his car with hurried instructions that she stay in the backyard, talk to no one, and he'd be right back.

Mrs. Entwhistle and Roger regarded the child on the other side of the fence. He was a stocky little boy, and Mrs. Entwhistle didn't think she could lift him up and over. While she wondered what to do, he toddled to a wide spot in the corner and squeezed through a gap with the nonchalance of repeated practice.

"Well, what about that?" Mrs. Entwhistle said. "You little booger, I bet you've done that before. Where in the world is that mama of yours? What's your name?"

But the child was unable or unwilling to reply.

"I'll call you Rocky," Mrs. Entwhistle said, "because it looks like you're between a rock and a hard place, wandering around alone at your age."

Mrs. Entwhistle devised a plan then and there. She'd take advantage of Pete's absence to use a neighbor's phone, notify the police to come and get the baby, call a cab and go home. Simple as that. These marshal people had obviously mistaken her for someone else, but she didn't seem to be having any luck convincing them of that, and she was tired of trying.

"I let myself be intimidated," she said. Talking aloud to herself had become a habit since her husband died. "Shame on me. But I won't continue to be such a spineless sap. I'm going home where I belong."

Pete would be back any minute. She had to hurry. Reaching down, she set the little fellow on his feet, took his hand and set out at his toddling pace to the neighbor's. But they hadn't gotten far when the slam of a car door announced Pete's return. She scurried back into the yard, Rocky and Roger in tow. She barely beat Pete, who arrived peering around the most enormous box of diapers Mrs. Entwhistle had ever seen.

"I went to Costco," Pete explained, reddening under her incredulous gaze. "It was the closest store, and I'm a member."

"Fine, Pete, fine. That ought to take care of Rocky for a while."

Freshly diapered, the baby began rubbing his eyes and yawning. "He needs a nap. I'm going to make him a pallet on the floor. It's better than nothing," Mrs. Entwhistle said.

Pete scooped up the baby, and they walked toward the house but he stopped so suddenly that Mrs. Entwhistle ran right into the back of him.

"For goodness sake, Pete, watch where—"

Something about the rigid set of Pete's neck silenced her. She followed his gaze to a black car with dark windows rolling slowly down the street. The deliberate pace and hidden occupants spoke menace. Pete thrust Rocky at her and said, "Get inside and lock the door behind you. Don't open up for anyone but me."

Gone was the hesitant young man who'd meekly shopped for diapers. She obeyed. This obedience thing is getting to be a habit, she thought, and look where it's gotten me. She waited, not even daring to peek out of the window, until Pete knocked on the back door.

"It's Deputy Marshal Pete Peters," he said formally. "You can open the door."

"How do I know it's you?" Mrs. Entwhistle asked, not above toying with pompous young people. "Slide your I.D. under the door."

There was a pause, during which she heard Pete muttering. A laminated card slid under the door.

"Okay, then," she said, sliding the dead bolt and turning the knob. "What the heck was all that about?"

"I have orders to move you, ma'am," said Pete, all business.

"Move me where? Why don't you just take me home? And what are you going to do about this baby?"

They both looked down at Rocky, who had fallen asleep on the floor and was drooling into the threadbare carpet. Roger stretched out, exhausted, beside him. Both were snoring lightly. Pete shook his head.

"I don't know," he said.

~*~

In the end, they took Rocky along. Pete said he'd call Child Protective Services as soon as they got to their destination. The baby didn't even wake when he was carried to the car and placed carefully on the back seat.

"You'll get arrested yourself if you get caught with a baby not strapped into a car seat," Mrs. Entwhistle said. She remembered the wild old days when her own children rode rampant, climbing over the seats and sticking their heads out of the windows. Sometimes she'd have to stop the car to spank them when they got too unruly. Car seats were a definite improvement as far as she was concerned.

"It can't be helped. We don't have time for that now. Get in, please."

"Wait. Roger has to go."

63

"We are going."

"No, I mean he has to *go*!"

This took some time, causing Pete to pace and look at his watch, but finally they were underway. Pete's eyes darted between the road ahead and the rearview mirror. Clearly nervous, he made Mrs. Entwhistle nervous, too. She tried again.

"Look, Pete, just drop me off at my house. I'm not your witness. There's been a mistake somewhere along the line and you've picked up the wrong person."

But Pete wasn't listening. He'd spotted the black car again, coming up fast behind them. "Hang on!" he said, putting his foot down hard. Rocky slid off the back seat onto the floor and started crying. Roger barked in sympathy. Mrs. Entwhistle turned and tried to reach over the seat to comfort the baby, but the car was rocking and rolling at such speed she couldn't keep her balance.

"Slow down, Pete, you're going to get us all killed," she roared.

"That's exactly what I'm trying to avoid!"

Pete executed a series of hairpin turns, darted through a red light and zipped through an alley so narrow that he left the passenger-side mirror behind. Spotting an open garage, he drove in, jumped out and punched the button that closed the door. They all blinked in the sudden gloom, and even Rocky stopped crying and stuck his thumb in his mouth.

Mrs. Entwhistle broke the silence. "Do you know these people?" she asked.

"You mean the people whose garage this is?

Whose house we're sort of breaking and entering? Why, no, I do not."

Pete had a wild look in his eyes and seemed on the verge of hysterics. Mrs. Entwhistle recognized that look as the same one Tommy used to get when he became overwrought. No good ever came of giving in to that. She spoke calmly.

"Well, all right, then. I'm sure they'll understand that it was an emergency. They're probably all at work anyway...."

She broke off in mid-sentence as the door connected to the house flew open, revealing a very young boy holding a very big gun. It was pointed directly at Mrs. Entwhistle.

"Stop, or I'll shoot!" the boy said. "Don't you try nothin'."

Mrs. Entwhistle was annoyed. She'd had about all the aggravation she could handle in one twenty-four hour period and the day was far from over.

"You put that gun down this minute, young man," she said. "You might hurt yourself, and you know very well you are not allowed to touch any of your father's guns when he's not home."

"It's not real," the boy said. "It's just a rep-repi-ca, Dad said. But it looks real, don't it?" He dropped the gun with a plasticky clatter.

"That's better. Now we'd like to come in, if you don't mind. We've got this baby, you see."

She looked around for Rocky, but he was heading into the house with the assurance of one who'd been there before. The resident boy looked at the toddling boy with astonishment.

"Joey? What are you doing here?" he said.

"Do you know this baby?" Mrs. Entwhistle asked.

"Sure, that's Joey. He's my sister's baby. Why do you have him?"

"Pete, where are we? Surely, we're far from where this baby belongs," Mrs. Entwhistle said.

"Actually, we made a big circle getting away from the car that was following us. We're on the back side of the block where the safe house is," Pete said.

"And you know this baby?" Mrs. Entwhistle asked again.

"Like I said, that's my nephew, Joey. Where's my sister? She works nights, but her boyfriend watches Joey while she sleeps."

"Nobody was watching him when I found him," Mrs. Entwhistle said grimly. "Anybody could have taken him. Lucky for him it was me."

"I'd better call my sister. She'll go nuts if Joey's not there when she wakes up."

"You can't call anyone, son," Pete said, clearing his throat and squaring his shoulders. "You're officially under the protection of the U.S. Marshal Service now, and I can't allow communication on any device."

"She probably wouldn't hear the phone anyway. She sleeps like she's dead," the boy said. "But you better get Joey back before she misses him, or I'm not kidding, she'll go nuts."

"What's your name, young man?" Mrs. Entwhistle inquired.

"Jack."

"Pleased to meet you, Jack. I'm Mrs. Entwhistle, and this is Marshal Peters. He's a good guy, so don't be scared."

Pete looked like he was scared himself. In fact, he looked like he was about to cry. Mrs. Entwhistle gave him a reassuring thump on the back. Pete jumped a foot at the unexpected touch and whirled around to see who was attacking him. Mrs. Entwhistle ignored this display of nerves. He was a grown man and a government agent, after all. In her opinion, he was responsible for this whole mess, and he could just darn well buck up. However, since he was clearly in a vulnerable state, it might not hurt to try to influence him again.

"It's time for you to take me home now, Pete," she said with all the authority of her seventy-eight years. She looked him straight in the eye, a double death-ray Mom Glare. Predictably, he quaked before it.

"Ma'am, I really can't do that," he said miserably.

"Pete, there's been a bad mistake made somewhere up the line. Not you, you're just following orders. But somebody has mistaken me for the witness in this trial you keep talking about. What if, while you're protecting me, the real witness gets hurt? Or, for that matter, what if I get hurt? Imagine the headlines: Elderly Woman Killed in Witness Protection Mix-Up. Whose record would that go on? I'm betting yours, not the big bosses, right?"

"You're right about that part, anyway," Pete said.

"But I can't just countermand an order when I'm out in the field."

"This is your chance to show you have initiative – leadership. I bet you'll be a hero. After all, I'm being held against my will. I believe that's called kidnapping. Again, who do you think will take the blame for that? You need to drop me off at home, and then go and get this whole thing straightened out."

"But what about the baby? We can't just leave these kids alone."

"Jack, what time will your parents be home?" Mrs. Entwhistle asked.

"Not until five-thirty," Jack said. "But Joey and me could go to my sister's house. She'll wake up if I shake her good. Then when my folks come home, she can bring me back. Oh boy, she's going to be in truuuuuuuble!"

Pete wiped a hand over his tired face as he thought over his options. He suddenly looked very young. Mrs. Entwhistle waited in silence. She knew enough about men to know you can only push so far.

"Look, I have to check in with headquarters," he finally said.

"You already know what they'll say," Mrs. Entwhistle said. "You're in this mess because you're following orders from people that have got it wrong."

Pete paced. He gazed out the window. Finally, he turned to Mrs. Entwhistle with a look of resolve.

"You're right," he said. "Let's get you home. I'll deal with the consequences."

~*~

Mrs. Entwhistle's house looked different, somehow. She felt as though she'd been gone for days instead of a few hours. Not a soul stirred on her street. Doors and windows wore a shuttered, unfriendly look. Pete helped her out of the car, holding Roger's leash while she paused for a moment to give her knees time to decide to move. Later she thought if she'd had younger knees, Pete wouldn't have gotten shot.

The same car with the ominously-tinted windows came screeching around the corner. Pete shoved her so hard that she fell full length across the front seat, whacking her head hard on the steering wheel. Roger let out an indignant yelp as Pete stepped on his tail. There was a sound like a car back-firing, and Mrs. Entwhistle felt little glass pellets rain down upon her. Then the car was gone.

With difficulty, she pulled herself up, head spinning, and brushed the glass out of her hair. But where was Pete? Roger's rusty bark directed her gaze downward, and she saw Pete lying half under the car on his back in a horrifying pool of dark red blood. Mrs. Entwhistle pressed her hands to her spinning head and willed the world to hold still. She knelt.

"Pete! Peter Peters," she said, her voice even louder than usual because she was scared.

Pete's eyes opened, but they looked glassy and uncomprehending. "Don't you die, now, you hear me? Don't be ridiculous. You're going to be all right."

Neighbors were coming out of their houses, gathering around the car. Several people were on their cell phones calling 911. Pete gave a long sigh and then – nothing. Without pausing to think, Mrs. Entwhistle tipped his head back, opened his mouth, bent over and blew a long steady breath into his mouth. She waited a few seconds and did it again, rewarded this time by the sight of Pete's chest rising. Pressing the heels of her hands into his sternum, she began rapid compressions.

Through the adrenalin rush, she heard the sirens coming closer. Time stopped as she concentrated on counting rapidly to one hundred, her hands keeping time. In a few seconds or a few days, strong hands lifted her out of the way, and blue-uniformed paramedics took over. One continued compressions while two more lifted Pete onto a stretcher and into the back of the ambulance.

Mrs. Entwhistle sat on the grass beside Roger, suddenly feeling that her legs wouldn't hold her. Ronnie Sue from next door helped her to her feet and retrieved her cane from where it fallen in the street. She walked Mrs. Entwhistle slowly to her door.

"Come on, Roger," Ronnie Sue said. "You're home."

~*~

"So then what happened?" Maxine asked, breathless with second-hand excitement. She'd rushed right over with homemade vegetable soup when Mrs. Entwhistle called. Maxine believed in the restorative powers of soup and always had a pot simmering. "And how did you know how to do CPR, anyway? Did you take a course?"

Mrs. Entwhistle shook her head. "But I watch a lot of television – cop shows, you know. Saw it done a hundred times. Nothing to it, really," she said modestly.

"And will Pete be okay?"

70

"So they tell me. He's being called a hero for saving my life, but honestly, I saved his life just as much as he did mine. Pete'll probably get a medal, but those Marshals are trying to forget I ever existed. They're just hoping I won't sue them for false arrest or something. Which I could, maybe, but I won't. Life's too short for that kind of aggravation."

"What about the real witness?" Maxine asked.

"It's all a big secret until after the trial. When those television guys came around I looked right into the camera and said that Cora Entwhistle is not a material witness to anything. Do you think I'll be on the eleven o'clock news tonight?"

"Probably," Maxine said. "Let's stay up late and watch it together."

"Diane and Tommy will have a hissy fit if they see me on the news before I've told them about it" Mrs. Entwhistle said. "And I know what's coming: lectures about staying home and keeping out of trouble. How was it my fault, I'll say to them. I was just hanging out sheets, minding my own business."

"For a change," Maxine said with a wink. "What about those little kids?"

"That nekkid baby and gun-toting boy? They're all right, although I bet that baby's mama got a good scolding from her own mama. 'Boyfriend was watching him', indeed," she said with a snort. "Boyfriends typically don't make very good baby-sitters; you'd think women would figure that out."

Maxine nodded with pursed lips. She and Mrs. Entwhistle could go on for hours about the general stupidity and ineptitude of the younger generation.

"I'll tell you one thing, Maxine," Mrs. Entwhistle said, "being in witness protection is a wearisome task. It just flat tuckers a person out. Come on and help me get my sheets in off the line before it gets dark. Aren't they going to smell good, after a whole day in the sunshine!"

Mrs. Entwhistle Tries Yoga

Her back hadn't been the same since she slipped going down the basement stairs. In fact, it hurt like the dickens. When her feet went out from under her, she'd sat down hard on the step, bumping her head on the railing and wrenching her back. Her head ached for days but that finally cleared up on its own. Mrs. Entwhistle firmly believed in applying tincture of time to all indispositions she might suffer. No good came from running to doctors' offices. And no good came from confessing mishaps like this one to her children, Diane and Tommy. Their solution to all problems was for her to move to an apartment in a senior living complex. Nothing wrong with that, but she wasn't ready. She loved the old-fashioned house where she'd spent her entire adult life, she loved her garden, her clothesline, her dog, - and yes, even her hard-to-reach basement, where she could stack plastic storage tubs until the cows came home.

But her back throbbed and kept throbbing, sending sharp arrows of pain down her left leg. Walking Roger was a chore, and she'd had to hire Ronnie Sue to do a little cleaning. This was not done to her standards, but she didn't say anything. The poor child couldn't know what she'd never been taught, and she was still a better option than asking Diane. At least Ronnie Sue's help didn't come with a lecture.

Pain had been her constant companion for six weeks. That morning when she'd rolled carefully out of bed and attempted to stand, it sent her to her knees. Roger whimpered while she clawed her way up the bedpost and onto her feet. It was time to go to the doctor. With an exasperated sigh, she picked up the phone and dialed.

"If you are experiencing a medical emergency, please hang up and dial 911. If you know your party's extension, please dial it now. Please listen carefully, for our options have changed. If you are a doctor or are calling from a doctor's office, please press one. If you are a pharmacy, please press two. If you wish to make an appointment, please press three..."

Mrs. Entwhistle pressed three.

"If you wish to make an appointment to see Dr. Effinger, please press one. If you wish to make an appointment to see Dr. Johnson or Dr. Ippolitto, please press two. If you wish to speak to a nurse, please leave a message and your call will be returned."

Mrs. Entwhistle pushed two.

"All of our representatives are busy helping other callers. Please leave your name, phone number and date of birth, and your call will be returned in the order in which it was received. Please do not leave multiple messages

74

as this slows the process."

"Cora Entwhistle, 824-6993. 6-1-1938." She was annoyed, which always raised her decibel level.

Her late husband, Floyd, used to say, "Cora don't really need a telephone. Her voice is so loud, she could just open a window and shout in the general direction." She never found him nearly as funny as he thought he was. When his attempts at humor didn't get a reaction, he'd launch into detailed explanations. She'd say, "Just because I'm not laughing doesn't mean I don't get it, Floyd." It made her smile to remember that now.

~*~

In due time, she presented herself in the office of Dr. Johnson, orthopedic surgeon. First came an x-ray, and only after this was in hand did the doctor enter the examining room where she waited. After a distracted greeting, he seated himself at the computer. His eyes never left the screen as he asked questions and typed in her answers.

"Does the pain keep you from doing your daily activities?" he finally asked.

"Only when the regular pole-dancer is sick and I have to fill in," Mrs. Entwhistle replied.

Dr. Johnson's head snapped up and for the first time he saw the elderly woman before him as a complete human being instead of a sore back. He grinned and looked ten years younger.

"Okay, I deserved that," he said. "I never thought, when I went to medical school that I'd end up a typist, but that's how things are now. Let's take a look at you."

When he finished, he said, "You've got a sore back."

Mrs. Entwhistle looked at him silently and raised one eyebrow.

"It'll get better eventually. I can give you an injection of cortisone if you like. Sometimes that helps some people. Or you can try physical therapy to stretch and strengthen the muscles around the injury. But what I'd really recommend is yoga."

"Yoga? You mean that twisty, pretzely thing?" she asked.

"There are different kinds of yoga. My wife does Hatha and my daughter swears by Bikram. You'd want to take a gentle stretching class for senior citizens."

"Oh, yes? I'm exceptionally limber for my age." Mrs. Entwhistle cherished a secret spark of pride because she could still bend down and touch her toes.

"Well, I suggest you look into classes and make sure you get a teacher who understands back injuries."

~*~

Mrs. Entwhistle discussed it with her best friend, Maxine. "Where would I find a yoga class? What would I wear? Would I be the only older person in a class full of kids?"

As usual, Maxine was a fount of reassuring information. "Why, start with the YWCA, Cora," she said, "I believe they have regular classes. And just wear slacks with some give to them. I wouldn't buy any special clothes until you see if you like it. I'd go with you, but my hip, you know."

"I know, Max. I'll figure it out."

~*~

The YWCA had a class called "Chair Yoga" for people with mobility issues. Some of them were in wheelchairs. Mrs. Entwhistle tried it: raise your right foot, raise your left foot, blah, blah. She was bored.

She peeked into another class on her way out. Soft lighting illuminated a large room filled with colorful yoga mats. On the mats were motionless bodies laid out like the dead. The instructor sat cross-legged at the front of the room, talking to the corpses in a soft voice.

"Relax your toes…relax your ankles…relax your calves…" she said. After the whole body had been traversed, she held up a large metal bowl and stroked it with a little stick. A wavering sound filled the room.

"Return to the breath," she said, "and begin to wiggle your fingers and toes. Do any stretch that your body may be calling for."

The corpses obediently wiggled and stretched.

"Pull your knees into your chest, hug your shins and rock back and forth. Roll onto your favorite side and rest in the fetal position for a few minutes. Now extend your top leg and push yourself to a sitting position with your hands. Sit with legs crossed and eyes closed, hands at your heart center. Bow your head over your heart. Namaste."

"Namaste," the group replied peacefully.

This is more like it, thought Mrs. Entwhistle. If I'm going to do yoga, I'm going to do real yoga.

Next day, she was there in her brown polyester pants topped with one of Floyd's old tee shirts. She noticed that everyone else was barefoot and togged out in colorful yoga outfits. She quickly slipped off her shoes. I'll have to see if I can find that old bottle of red nail polish that Diane left in her room, and paint my toes, she thought. If I come again.

The instructor said her name was Carmen. She introduced Mrs. Entwhistle to the class, and the other members, all of whom looked to be on the sunny side of thirty, smiled and nodded.

"I have a bad back," Mrs. Entwhistle announced. "My doctor told me to try yoga for the stretching."

"That's fine," Carmen said. "Do only what feels good. Listen to your body."

"Can't help but listen, my back's been yelling," Mrs. Entwhistle said. Carmen's beatific smile never wavered.

Mrs. Entwhistle took a bright orange mat from the stack, unrolled it on the hardwood floor and looked down at it. With a little help from the wall, she lowered herself to the floor inch by inch, but sitting cross-legged made her left leg go into spasm. Carmen showed her how to sit in Staff position, legs extended, toes pointing up and spine straight. It was harder than it looked. Her thighs quivered with the effort. She tried to quell her competitive instincts by telling herself that she couldn't be expected to be as agile as all those youngsters. There was some comfort in knowing that she was the oldest person in the room by at least forty years.

Class began with meditation and breathing exercises. Mrs. Entwhistle liked letting her mind bat away random thoughts like thistledown. She enjoyed breathing in to a count of eight, hooolding it, and breathing out to a count of ten. By golly, her lungs still worked as well as anybody's.

Then the twisting began. She watched the others carefully and tried to do what they did. Cat/Cow felt good; Child's Pose was not easy on old knees. Sun Salutes, Warriors, Yoga Mudra — it was all new territory and she navigated it with her usual determination.

Carmen came over to whisper, "Relax, Cora. Don't try to push through the poses, just let them happen. There's no right way or wrong way."

Some of what Carmen directed the class to do was just plain stupid, in Mrs. Entwhistle's opinion. Happy Baby, for instance, was embarrassing. No way was she exposing her personal parts like that. She couldn't even look at the others while they were doing it.

Class ended with what Carmen called Savasana. She turned down the lights and they all stretched out on their backs, just like the corpses Mrs. Entwhistle had observed the day before. Chanting from the CD player softly filled the room. Carmen distributed little bean bags she called eye pillows. She placed one gently over Mrs. Entwhistle's eyes. Mrs. Entwhistle relaxed.

Her own snoring woke her with a start. Embarrassed, she raised her head and glanced around the room to see if anyone else had heard. But the room was empty. All the mats were rolled up and piled neatly in the corner. The lights were turned off. Only Mrs. Entwhistle remained in the dim room.

"Stretched out on the floor like a dead mackerel,"

she said aloud. "And not only that, I'm not sure I can get up."

Gingerly, she raised herself to one elbow and pushed to a sitting position. Curling her legs under her, she managed to get to her knees; hanging onto the wall, she scrambled to her feet.

"Hey, my back doesn't hurt," she said to the empty room. "One class and my back doesn't hurt. I must be a natural."

Bending over to roll up and replace her mat did give her a twinge or two, but on the whole, she felt remarkably loose. The miserable tightness that had tormented her for weeks was gone. She headed to the locker room to collect her purse. It took her a few moments to work the combination lock and while she was at it, she overheard a conversation on the other side of the wall of lockers.

"Did you see that old lady?" a female voice said.

"She was a game old bird, wasn't she?"

"Passed out during Savasana. I wonder what Carmen did about that?"

"She let me sleep," Mrs. Entwhistle said. There was dead silence. Then two sleek blonde heads peered around the corner.

"We're so sorry!" one of them said. "We really admire you for trying yoga. At your age."

"You'll get old, too, believe it or not," Mrs. Entwhistle said.

The blonder of the two said, "Are you having trouble with your lock? Can I help?"

"I can do it," Mrs. Entwhistle said firmly, and she did. Retrieving her purse, she left the building, surprised to find that day had faded into soft summer dusk. The two young women fell into step beside her as they walked to the parking lot.

"I'm Tiffany, and this is Chrissie."

"Cora Entwhistle."

"Look, we're really sorry for being so rude. We're going to Starbucks for coffee. May we buy you a cup, to apologize?"

"Do they have tea at this place?"

"They do."

"What about how I'm dressed?" Mrs. Entwhistle looked down at Floyd's tee shirt and her old brown slacks. The girls wore black, skin-tight yoga pants and low-cut tops.

"Oh, whatever. It doesn't matter." Left hanging in the air was the rest of the sentence: "at your age."

Cautioning herself not to be tiresomely over-sensitive, Mrs. Entwhistle weighed the prospect of making new, young friends against the tug of home and sofa. Don't be an old poop, she counseled herself.

"All right, then. I'll come."

~*~

Tiffany waited until they had their beverages of choice and were seated at an outside table. Then she dug into her purse and pulled out a foil-wrapped square, waving it enticingly under Chrissie's nose.

"Oh, you bad girl, what have you done?" Chrissie said, her eyes wide.

"Shhhh! Just a little baking. Want to share?"

"Mmmmm, I sure do!"

Mrs. Entwhistle couldn't understand what the fuss was about. Unwrapped, the little brown squares looked like perfectly ordinary brownies. Young people could make such a production out of the simplest things, like they were the first women in history to bake brownies. Probably from a mix, too.

"Mrs. Entwhistle – Cora – care to try a brownie?" Tiffany said, a devilish twinkle in her eye.

"Tiffany! Mrs. Entwhistle is too old..."

Mrs. Entwhistle immediately took the proffered square, popped most of it in her mouth and chewed. The brownie tasted a tad off, she thought. Maybe she'd suggest, just to be helpful, that Tiffany try a caramel drizzle over the next batch. Floyd had loved that. The young women watched her, suppressing giggles and rolling their eyes at each other. Why, she couldn't fathom. What was so funny about eating a brownie? These girls made the biggest deal over nothing. She ate the last bite and sipped her tea. Tiffany and Chrissie finished their brownies, too, and lolled back in their chairs. No one spoke for a while, but it was a comfortable silence. A feeling of mellow relaxation stole over Mrs. Entwhistle. She felt that she could sit there all night, listening to the gentle hum of conversation around them, thinking about nothing.

Tiffany finally spoke. "Oh, wow, look at the stars," she said. "So many. One, two, three, four...uh, a hundred.

I love stars. I just looooove stars, and they just looooove me."

Chrissie found this remark extremely funny and laughed so hard she got hiccups. Mrs. Entwhistle smiled fondly at her new friends. Such light-hearted young ladies. They were being kind to her, sharing their little treats and all. She leaned her head back to look at the stars, too, but the world spun and the sky looked like someone had scribbled across it with a silver pen.

"Whooee," Mrs. Entwhistle said softly. She felt like laughing and maybe crying a little bit, too. Memories of Floyd floated through her head - not the Floyd of old age, paunchy and cranky, but Floyd when she'd first met him, strong, slender and masterful. Remembering the things she and Floyd got up to back then made her face burn. She looked around anxiously to see if anyone had noticed.

"I was married for fifty-four years," she announced, peering at the girls owlishly. It seemed important to tell them that. "I'm single, now. Well, I'm a widow. Widows are single, aren't they? Maybe there's an age limit, though. I might be too old to be single."

"I don't think you are," Chrissie said. She wrinkled her brow in the effort to give the matter serious consideration. "Single means not married, and you're not married so... I guess you're single."

"Do you ever date?" Tiffany asked.

"Date what?"

"You know, like, a guy."

"A guy? Oh, no. I have Roger. He's guy enough for me."

"Oho! Roger! You're holding out on us!"

"No, no, Roger is, well, he is a male, but…"

Mrs. Entwhistle couldn't quite put her finger on what Roger was. She thought a minute.

"He's a dog!" she finished triumphantly.

"They're all dogs!" Chrissie said, and the girls again went off into gales of laughter. Mrs. Entwhistle smiled politely.

"Speaking of Roger, I've got to get home," she said. "It's past his supper time. He gets upset if I'm late with his supper."

"Yeah, he's male, all right," Tiffany said.

"Now, where did I leave my car?"

Mrs. Entwhistle pondered. Had she walked to this place? She couldn't remember. She stood but had to catch the table to keep from staggering.

"I must be more tired from that yoga class than I thought," she said.

"Mrs. Entwhistle, I don't think you want to drive right now," Chrissie said. "Let's call you a cab."

"Ta-da, she's a cab!" Tiffany said, and had to put her head down on the table, her shoulders shaking with laughter.

Chrissie pulled out her phone and punched in a number. Mrs. Entwhistle thought of protesting, but she did feel very unsteady on her feet. Maybe it would be better to take a taxicab home and then ask Maxine to drive her back to the Y to pick up the car tomorrow. That was probably where she'd left it. She sat back down, feeling a no-reason smile spreading across her face.

"Gosh, I'm hungry again," she said. "Sleepy, too. Yoga sure is relaxing."

"Are you going to come to class again?" Chrissie asked, winking at Tiffany.

"Oh, no, I don't think so," Mrs. Entwhistle said, around a huge yawn. "I think I've pretty well cured what ailed me."

Mrs. Entwhistle Writes an Advice Column

Maxine was finally going to have her hip replaced. Mrs. Entwhistle knew it had been bothering her for ages, but she'd put it off as long as she could.

"I just hate the idea of going under the knife," Maxine would say mournfully, when she had to be helped gently up from a chair or when she switched to a quad cane to keep her balance.

"Well, Max, nobody wants to," Mrs. Entwhistle would respond. "But you aren't getting any younger and recovery just gets more difficult as we age."

The orthopedic surgeon said Maxine would be ready when the pain overcame the fear, and that was the case. Now she was preparing herself. Deep-watering her flower beds, washing all her clothes, putting fresh sheets on the bed and making a big pot of vegetable soup for the freezer so she wouldn't have to cook right away when she came home. Not that she would have, anyway, because Mrs. Entwhistle would take care of her meals for a while. But that was Max. Always thinking ahead.

"The thing is," Max said, "I don't know what I'll do about my column in the Senior Times."

Max wrote an advice column in a little neighborhood newspaper that you could pick up free outside the supermarket. It was mostly ads, but there was Maxine's column, a gardening column written by a gentleman who raised prize peonies and also raised hell if a child's ball rolled into his yard, and a recipe column. All were written anonymously, but Maxine knew the other columnists from chance meetings in the publisher's office when she dropped off her copy.

Maxine's column was called "Ask a Senior," which Mrs. Entwhistle privately thought was a dumb title. Most of the questions were sent in by readers, but Maxine admitted confidentially that sometimes when the mail was light, she had to make up both the question and the answer. She loved the column, however, and spent a lot of time earnestly researching her answers and agonizing over her advice. Since her pay was exactly nothing and she had no byline, Mrs. Entwhistle found it puzzling that she spent so much time and effort. But she knew it was important to her friend, and so she listened respectfully to her worries.

"I just don't know if I'll feel like writing while I'm recovering. When I had my gall bladder out two years ago, I couldn't think straight for the longest time. The doctor said anesthesia can do that sometimes. And I'll have to go to rehab for a while this time. It'll be hard to concentrate there. I'd hate to give advice that wasn't well thought-out."

Mrs. Entwhistle wondered if anyone would notice, since Maxine's writing style was so fluttery and full of kind euphemisms that it was hard to locate the advice at all. But her dearest and oldest friend was worrying about something that Mrs. Entwhistle could easily fix.

"I'll do it," she said.

"Oh, um, Cora, do you think you could? Or would want to, I mean?"

"Of course I can do it," Mrs. Entwhistle said with her customary self-confidence when presented with a challenge. "I'll write what I'd say if I were talking to you."

Maxine looked worried, but she agreed. She almost always agreed with whatever Mrs. Entwhistle proposed. And so Mrs. Entwhistle found herself getting the mail at the post office box rented especially for this purpose on the second day of Max's hospitalization. Sure enough, there were two letters addressed to "Ask a Senior." She took the envelopes home, slit the first, removed the lined sheet of paper and perused the spidery writing.

"Dear Ask a Senior, I am eighty-six years of age and living on what my husband and I saved while we were working. I don't have a great deal of money, but I have plenty for my needs, which are few. What is the fair thing to do when one of your adult children needs money and you have some to spare, but the other children, who don't need it, resent you giving it? Should one make provisions in one's will so that the child you helped gets less of an inheritance? Or give equal amounts now to all the children, even those who don't need it? (I really couldn't afford to do that.) Or should I lend the money and get a promissory note? It seems so mean to demand that of one's own child. What should I do? Signed, Worried Mother."

"Easy peasy," Mrs. Entwhistle said aloud.

She wrote, *"Dear Worried Mother. This is your money, right? Money that you worked for and saved over the years. You can do exactly as you please with it and you needn't explain yourself to anyone, let alone your children. Let them haggle over your estate after you're gone and don't have to hear about it. While you're alive, you get to decide. Stop listening to your children complain. What do they know, anyway?"*

She reread her reply and thought it was just right. The second letter was from a man.

Dear Senior, My wife has a little car that is ten years old. It runs pretty good, but it needs to have regular maintenance, especially oil changes. She NEVER thinks about getting this done. There is a little sticker right on the windshield where she can't help but see it that clearly says the date for the next oil change. Does she do it? NO. I am thinking of selling her car because she isn't a responsible owner. Signed, Oil-Can Harry.

Mrs. Entwhistle had to step outside and pace around the yard for a few minutes, until her blood stopped boiling. When she returned to the house, she wrote:

Dear Oil-Can, Why don't you put a dunce cap on her head and seat her in the corner while you're at it? Let's see now: who launders your clothes and returns them to your closet? Do you ever think about doing that? Who decides what to fix for supper, goes to the market and prepares the food? Do you ever think about doing that? Who remembers your kids' birthdays and buys cards and presents? Do you ever think about doing that? Who makes the appointments for your physicals and dental check-ups? Do you ever think about doing that? Oil-Can, you are fortunate your wife lets you sleep in the house. Count your blessings, change her oil and shut up."

That was fun, Mrs. Entwhistle thought. This column business has more to it than meets the eye.

~*~

She checked the post office box every day, but no more letters came. The column was due to be turned in on Tuesday, and on Monday when she made her daily visit to Max in rehab, she asked if two letters would be enough. She seemed to remember that Max's column was longer than that.

"Sometimes there is a dry spell," Maxine said. Her face was flushed with a touch of fever, which the nurse assured them was nothing to worry about. But Mrs. Entwhistle did worry, because it meant Maxine had to miss her physical therapy until she was better, and that was the whole point of enduring this semi-awful place.

It really wasn't so bad, Mrs. Entwhistle admitted, trying to be fair. It was clean, staff was friendly, if overly-busy, and the physical therapy was getting Max back on her feet. But how much better to be home in your own place, sleeping in your own bed, eating what you felt hungry for instead of what was on your tray. Mrs. Entwhistle brought Max one good meal a day, cooked in her own kitchen and transported as quickly as possible in the hope of serving it warm. It made Mrs. Entwhistle remember her stint with Meals on Wheels.

Now she shook out a cloth napkin over Maxine's bedside tray and placed a plate containing a pork chop, mashed potatoes with a little well of brown gravy, green beans from her garden, cooked with bacon, and a yeast roll from the batch she'd made this morning.

"Blackberry cobbler for dessert," she said, watching as Maxine made a valiant effort to look hungry. "Here, let me cut up the pork chop for you."

"It looks and smells delicious," Maxine said. "You are so dear to bring me this nice meal. But…I guess the fever has taken my appetite."

"Just drink the sweet tea, then. You must stay hydrated." Mrs. Entwhistle took a few bites herself. She was starving.

"So what do you do when you don't get enough questions for the column?" she asked.

"You know, I sometimes have to fabricate a question. I always try to make it something I've heard my friends talk about," Maxine said.

"Okay, let's brain-storm. How about: 'Dear Ask a Senior, I am thinking of having an affair. Is it true you have to buy new underwear?'"

"Oh, Cora!" Maxine looked tickled and shocked at once. "You couldn't put something so – racy – in the Senior Times!"

"Well, then, this: 'Dear Ask a Senior, My ex-husband wants me to sell his car and send him the money. Is a dollar too much to ask for the car?'"

By now Maxine was laughing. "I think I could eat a little now…oh, it's all gone."

"Here, you can have the cobbler," Mrs. Entwhistle said guiltily, handing it over.

Finally, they settled on a topic which they'd heard

discussed on an afternoon talk show. How do you keep the neighborhood dogs from using your shrubs for a urinal?

Maxine was in favor of putting up a cute little sign saying something like, "No doggies allowed" with a picture of a dear little puppy. Mrs. Entwhistle pointed out that dogs can't read. She advised sitting in wait on the porch with garden hose turned on jet spray. They compromised by suggesting that a large tin of red pepper ("Not too much money at Costco," Maxine said) be liberally sprinkled around the inviting shrubbery. Together, they composed their answer and Mrs. Entwhistle wrote it out in her beautiful cursive penmanship.

By the time Mrs. Entwhistle packed up her dinner basket and said goodbye, Maxine looked much better. The next day, Mrs. Entwhistle handed in her copy to the Senior Times editor.

~*~

"Did you see what Ask a Senior said to the guy who wanted to punish his wife by getting rid of her car?"

"Yes, it was hilarious! She really nailed him. Looks like Senior has developed a backbone."

Mrs. Entwhistle stopped her grocery cart in order to hear the conversation in the next aisle. The voices continued.

"And that poor old soul who worried about how to distribute her money between her grabby kids!"

"Yep, Senior nailed that one, too. You know, I've thought about that myself. Andy just can't seem to get it all together, and what am I supposed to do when he doesn't have a place to live, or his car breaks down and he can't get to work? Yet, Sarah and Jake act so ugly when I help…."

The voices faded as the shoppers moved on, but Mrs. Entwhistle remained transfixed. Feedback! Honest feedback from people who didn't even know they were giving it! No wonder authors got so hooked on writing. She wished they'd said something about how pepper worked as a dog-deterrent. Abandoning her shopping cart, she left the store and headed straight to the post office. Maybe there'd be another letter.

There were three. She ripped open the envelopes with eager fingers, reading them as she sat in the car.

"Dear Ask a Senior: Do you know how to get rust stains out of a porcelain sink?"

"Oh, for heaven's sake!" Mrs. Entwhistle said, wrinkling her nose in disbelief. "Anybody knows that. Barkeeper's Friend. Who would waste a stamp on such a dumb question?"

Dear Ask a Senorita: Where have you been all my life? Here's what I'd like to do to you….

Mrs. Entwhistle dropped that one like it was on fire. While she hadn't even heard of some of the proposed acts, she was pretty sure they were not appropriate for a lady of her advanced years. "Floyd would have a fit," she muttered to herself.

The third letter had been typed on a computer.

Dear Ask A Senior: My mom says I have to learn to write in cursive, even though my school doesn't teach it any longer. She says I won't be able to sign my name legally unless I learn it. I told her handwriting is no longer important because everything is done on the computer, and we'll soon sign with a thumbprint or an eyeball scan. How can I get her to see reason? The dark ages are over! Signed, Tired of Being Nagged.

Oh, this was one she could really get her teeth into! She whipped out her notebook and pen and wrote her response right there in the car.

Dear Nagged: You poor children are being short-changed by your schools. What if all the computers in the world stopped working? That isn't so far-fetched, is it? Who's going to scan your eyeball then? Decent penmanship is a skill, just like learning a foreign language, and it will be useful all your life. Ask your mother to sit down and show you how it's done and then practice until you get good at it. Write me another letter when you can do so in your own cursive hand.

~*~

Over the next few weeks, the letters increased from a tiny trickle to what felt like a torrent. Mrs. Entwhistle was amazed by the amount of advice she was expected to dish out on order. People wanted to know how to get ink stains out of a cotton shirt, what to do about noisy neighbors, where to find old-fashioned orange slice candy, when to neuter a puppy. They entreated her to tell them how to heal a rift between father and son, where to find a good nursing home for an ancient mother, what to do when an employee is caught stealing. Mrs. Entwhistle's desk light burned late as she dispensed advice in her inimitable style: short and not sweet.

It was finally time for Maxine to come home from her stay in the rehab center. Mrs. Entwhistle went to get her, and together they waited for the doctor to sign the discharge papers. They passed the time by reviewing the latest *Ask a Senior* letters.

"You'd have to be Solomon to answer some of these questions," Mrs. Entwhistle said. "I don't know how you've done it."

Maxine looked pensive.

"My, the letters have certainly come pouring in since you started writing the column," she said in a small voice. "I guess people will be disappointed when I take over again. Or maybe the editor won't want me back."

"Of course you'll take over your column again," Mrs. Entwhistle said. "I'm just a poor substitute and I'll be glad to give it back to you. Your advice is much nicer than mine."

"But maybe not as interesting."

"Well, then kick it up a notch, Maxine. You've lived long enough to say what you mean and mean what you say. Besides, nobody knows who writes the dang thing. You don't have to be so nice."

Maxine made no reply, but Mrs. Entwhistle didn't miss the speculative gleam in her eye. She slit the next envelope and read the letter aloud.

Dear Ask A Senior: My 85-year-old father-in-law lives with us. He orders pornographic movies on our cable connection. Aside from the fact that I find this disgusting, it brings me a swarm of porn e-mails which I fear contain viruses. When asking that he respect my wishes in this matter didn't work, I set up parental controls on his television set. Somehow he learned the PIN number and ordered another movie last night. I'm at my wit's end.

What should I do? Signed, Mary Poppins

Maxine stared thoughtfully at the ceiling as she pondered her reply. Mrs. Entwhistle's fingers fairly itched to seize paper and pen and compose the blistering response that was knocking around in her head. Please, please, Max, let him have it, she begged silently. Don't get all sweet and fluffy with the old goat.

Maxine had been her best friend for fifty years, and Mrs. Entwhistle felt the two of them were as close as sisters, but Max still had some surprises up her sleeve. She scratched out her reply and handed it wordlessly to Mrs. Entwhistle, who read:

Dear Mary: This man isn't going to change his stripes at 85. Maybe he has a touch of dementia or maybe he's just ornery. In either case, you must take charge, as you would with a rebellious teenager. Remove the cable box from his television set. Tell him that since he finds it impossible to comply with the house rules on his own, you will help him by removing temptation. Don't relent. Network television is the fate he chose for himself.

A smile slowly spread across Mrs. Entwhistle's face as she read. "Maxine, that's the perfect solution. How did you get to be so wise?"

"You would have thought of the same thing eventually," Maxine said modestly.

"You know me better than that," Mrs. Entwhistle said. "I'd have eviscerated him."

"I've got a letter here that I think is meant for you," Maxine said, handing it over.

Mrs. Entwhistle saw it was addressed in large, childish handwriting. It said:

Dear Ask a Senior: You said to write a letter back in cursive. Well, here it is. I've been practicing and it's getting easier. My best friend is learning to do it, too. The other kids can't even read cursive, so it's like we have our own secret code. Thanks.

"Well, swanee," Mrs. Entwhistle said. "I really didn't expect to hear from her again. Good for her."

"And good for you, Cora," Maxine said. "You made a difference to that child."

"Oh, now," Mrs. Entwhistle said. She felt her cheeks grow warm, and quickly changed the subject. "Let's get you ready to go home."

Roger Gets Lost

Roger preferred the house. When necessity dictated, he'd waddle reluctantly to the back door and nudge the little bell that Mrs. Entwhistle had attached to the knob. She called it tinkling to tinkle. Roger often needed a cheering section to accomplish the deed: "Go potty, Roger, goooo on, gooood booooy." Having achieved success, he wasted no time getting back inside to the comfort of his favorite sofa pillow. So when Mrs. Entwhistle couldn't find him one Thursday afternoon, she was puzzled.

First, she checked his favorite haunts: the living room sofa, the guest room bed, the cool kitchen tiles. No Roger. Then she went into every room, looking under and behind furniture. No Roger.

The back door had been standing open to air out a little cooking mishap. She'd forgotten a skillet on the stove when she answered a phone call, and the cooking oil had smoked something awful. Hopefully, neither Diane nor Tommy would hear about it. Next thing you knew, they'd say she was too old to cook, just like when they'd decided she was too old to drive. Well, she'd fixed that. She'd taken a remedial driving course, and then she'd waved her certificate of competency under Tommy's nose until he'd brought back her Buick. After that, there were no more little fender-benders and no more sassy backtalk about driving from Diane and Tommy. But now - where could Roger have gotten to?

She checked the back yard, although it was highly unlikely he'd gone outside of his own volition. Mrs. Entwhistle was not one to panic, but she felt uneasy. She looked up and down the empty street. Ventured to the edge of the sidewalk and called his name. Ronnie Sue, from next door, heard her and came out.

"What's wrong, did Roger get away?" she asked.

"Roger doesn't typically go anywhere," Mrs. Entwhistle said, "but I can't seem to locate him just at the moment."

"Let me help you look for him," Ronnie Sue said. She and Roger had a special bond. She began calling his name in the high, squeaky voice that he absolutely loved. But there was no response.

"You walk that way and I'll walk this way," Ronnie Sue said, heading south.

Mrs. Entwhistle went north. Soon the neighborhood resounded with calls of "Roger! Roger!" The few neighbors who were home during the day joined the search. They covered a four-block area, but no one found Roger. Mrs. Entwhistle was seriously worried now.

"I'll make some posters," Ronnie Sue said. "Do you have any pictures of him?"

Of course, Mrs. Entwhistle had pictures. Lots of them. In a remarkably short time, Ronnie Sue and her computer had produced flyers with Roger's photo, name and address. LOST DOG, it said across the top. Mrs. Entwhistle's stomach gave a little lurch.

She backed her car carefully down the driveway and drove slowly in a wider circle than the foot search had encompassed. Maybe she'd spot him trotting down an unfamiliar sidewalk, lost and confused. Because Roger wasn't a street-smart dog. On their walks, he'd pull on the leash if he spotted a cat or a squirrel; he'd run right into the path of traffic if Mrs. Entwhistle didn't stop him.

Driving home, she saw Ronnie Sue had already tacked a number of posters on telephone poles. LOST DOG, they accused her. *How could you be so careless with your dear friend?* should have been the sub-text.

When she got home, Mrs. Entwhistle called Maxine.

"Oh, my goodness, poor little doggie!" Maxine said. She loved Roger, too. "I'll be right over."

And she was, arriving within fifteen minutes with her signature homemade soup. This batch was frozen solid. Maxine had a freezer full of soups. Today's was chicken noodle. That was no-fooling-around comfort food and denoted the depth of Maxine's concern.

"Have you called the police?" she asked Mrs. Entwhistle. "Or the fire station? They're good about helping with pets."

"No, I didn't even think of that." She went directly to the phone and dialed 911.

"What is your emergency?" the voice at the other end asked.

"I've got a lost dog," Mrs. Entwhistle said. "My dog, Roger, is gone and I can't find him anywhere."

"You need to call Animal Control for a lost dog," the voice said unsympathetically. "This line is for people."

"But couldn't you just ask the patrolmen to keep an eye out for a little lost-looking Shih 'Tzu?" Mrs. Entwhistle begged. "They're driving around anyway, and they might see him. If they did, they could call me and I'd go pick him up. Couldn't you just do that much?"

There was a pause. "I'm not supposed to. I could get in trouble, but I have a dog, too, and I know how you feel. Tell you what, I'll just radio the guys that are on patrol in your neighborhood and ask them to keep an eye out, okay?"

"Thank you so much," Mrs. Entwhistle said. "Roger's not used to being on his own."

Then they waited. Maxine and Mrs. Entwhistle sat on the front porch swing, and every few minutes one or the other of them would walk to the sidewalk and look up and down the street. Maxine thawed her soup, heated it and brought Mrs. Entwhistle a bowl, but it went untouched. It was getting dark. Roger had never been out in the dark alone. What would he do? Where would he

101

sleep? Would he curl up under a bush, or would he just walk all night? Had he already been hit by a car, his warm furry body cooling in a ditch somewhere? How would she ever know if that had happened? Roger had an engraved tag attached to his collar. It contained his name, address and phone number. Maybe someone would read that, and…

Mrs. Entwhistle had gone through Floyd's entire funeral without shedding a tear. Tears were private. But now she felt treacherous wetness in her eyes and an unmanageable lump in her throat. She couldn't speak. Maxine knew her old friend well, and there was no attempt at conversation. The swing moved gently back and forth.

It was almost dark. Fireflies were blinking in the yard, and cars had their headlights on when the phone rang. Mrs. Entwhistle sprang up so quickly she had to throw out a hand to steady herself on the wall. Her phone lived in a little niche in the front hall and she made her way to it as quickly as possible.

"Hello?"

"Is this 1229 Butterworth Drive?"

"Yes. Who's this?"

"Never mind who this is. You missing a little dog?"

"Yes! Do you know where he is? Do you have him?" She heard Roger's rusty bark. "You *do* have him. Where are you? I'll be right there to pick him up."

"Not so fast, lady. I found him, so don't I get a finder's fee or somethin'? A reward? Or else, if you don't wanna pay, I could keep him; use him for a bait dog. I got me some fightin' pit bulls that would just love to get at him."

Mrs. Entwhistle's legs gave way and she sat down suddenly on the little bench by the telephone. "Oh," she said faintly. "No. Roger can't fight. He's old. And small."

"He don't need to fight. He just needs to get 'et up." The caller laughed. "Unless you want to pay me my fee."

"What *is* your fee?"

"Oh, let's see. I'd say ten thou would be about right."

Mrs. Entwhistle could get her hands on ten thousand dollars. Just. It was in a money market account at the bank. She didn't hesitate. "I'll write you a check."

"Now, lady, really? You think I'm goin' into some bank and cashin' your personal check? No, gotta have cash."

"But the bank is closed and I can't get that much from the ATM."

"Hafta be tomorrow then, won't it? You go get the money first thing, and I'll call you again to set up a swap."

"But is Roger all right? Does he have food and water? Where will he sleep tonight?"

There was a click. The line went dead. Mrs. Entwhistle put her head between her knees until the room stopped spinning. Carefully, she made her way back to the porch, where Maxine waited.

"Some man has got Roger. He wants ten thousand dollars tomorrow morning," she said.

"Oh, my stars!" Maxine said. "Do you have it to spare? If you don't, I do. I'll give it to you."

That was so kind, so like Maxine, that Mrs. Entwhistle had to fight back tears for the second time that day. "No," she said, "but thank you. I've got it. Not to spare, exactly, but I'll pay it to get Roger back safely."

~*~

Maxine stayed over. Neither of the ladies went to bed; they dozed in the living room. Maxine lay on the sofa under a quilt, and Mrs. Entwhistle stretched out in Floyd's old recliner. Somehow, it was a comfort, that old chair. Almost like having his arms around her again.

Both of them were up long before dawn, making tea in the kitchen, rubbing their red eyes. Mrs. Entwhistle, though exhausted, felt energized because something else had happened during that long, wakeful night. She'd gotten mad.

"What that man is doing is a crime," she said.

"It sure is!" Maxine replied. "He's a lowdown skunk. But I don't know if kidnapping laws actually apply to dogs."

"No, I mean it's a criminal act. It's extortion. He's extorting money from me. I'll be damned if he's going to get away with it." Mrs. Entwhistle seldom swore, but Maxine had seen that look in her eyes on other occasions. It did not bode well for whoever crossed her. She waited to see what her friend would do next.

"I've been thinking it over all night," Mrs. Entwhistle continued. "The police may not take this seriously. They have a lot of crimes they may consider more pressing than a kidnapped dog. But I've got an alternative."

"What's that?"

"Pete Peters, Deputy U.S. Marshal!" Mrs. Entwhistle said triumphantly.

Mrs. Entwhistle met Pete when he was assigned to protect her during her incarceration (as she thought of it) in the Witness Protection Program. When he'd gotten shot, she'd saved his life by giving CPR until the ambulance arrived, and then she'd visited him frequently during his recuperation. They'd become friends. He'd said over and over that he owed her, and he showed up at her house from time to time to help with whatever tasks she could no longer accomplish herself. Yes, Pete was just the person to help her now. She had his number on speed-dial.

"Peters," said a sleepy voice.

"Cora Entwhistle, Pete."

"Mrs. Entwhistle? Good God, do you know what time it is? It isn't even light yet."

"I need your help. Somebody's got Roger."

"Got him? What do you mean?"

Mrs. Entwhistle told him.

"Okay. I'll be right there. Put the coffee on."

That meant Mrs. Entwhistle would have to dig out Floyd's old coffee-maker, seldom used since his death. But it was a small price to pay for the help of a Deputy U.S. Marshal.

Pete tapped at the kitchen door before putting his head in. "It's Pete," he announced unnecessarily. He entered, smiled at Maxine and pecked Mrs. Entwhistle on the cheek. "Tell me everything," he said, accepting a cup of coffee.

Mrs. Entwhistle related the whole story in detail. "So poor Roger has been gone all night," she finished, "and he's being threatened by pit bulls. He must be scared to death. I'll do whatever it takes to get him home, but I don't want that creep to get away with it."

"No," Pete said thoughtfully, and Mrs. Entwhistle could almost see his mind ticking over, sorting facts and planning action. Pete had improved a lot since their first encounter. Then, he'd been brand-new to the Marshal service, inexperienced and easily cowed. Now, he was a seasoned, decorated agent, although he'd never in a million years mention his medal. She felt better just because he was sitting in her kitchen, thinking.

"Do you have ten thousand dollars, and do you want to risk it for Roger?" Pete asked.

Mrs. Entwhistle looked at him. She nodded.

"Okay, I had to ask. Here's what I think we should do."

~*~

Mrs. Entwhistle carried a green canvas bag that said "Publix" on the side. In it was ten thousand dollars in twenties, as Roger's kidnapper had specified in his call that morning. Pete had protested, wanted her to fill the bag with shredded newspaper with some money on top, but she wouldn't do it. She couldn't take the chance. If their plan worked, she'd redeposit the money in the bank. If it didn't, it might be all that saved Roger's life.

She walked along the path in a deserted section of the park. Not much was going on at one p.m. on a Friday. School kids weren't out yet, and toddlers who'd filled the playground earlier were home taking their naps. When the path led into a small stand of trees, knowing that Pete was hiding nearby gave her the courage to keep walking. That and her anger. It had been simmering all day. Who was low enough to hold a lost dog for ransom, to scare an old lady (she could call herself that; no one else had better) and extort from her what little savings she had? She had a surprise up her sleeve and hoped she'd have the opportunity to use it.

Her steps slowed as she approached the white-painted rock set in a clearing among the trees. It was one of those rocks that got painted every year by graduating high school seniors. "Go Warriors! Class of '16" it said in big spray-painted letters. From behind it stepped a man. He wore a black tee shirt with an obscene message printed on it, and black jeans ripped at the knees. His hair was pulled back into a greasy bun. Mrs. Entwhistle didn't approve of man-buns, but it was the least of her disapprovals of this particular man.

"Have you got Roger?" she demanded, taking the initiative as Pete had instructed.

107

"You got the money?"

"I have to see Roger first."

Man-Bun jerked on a length of rope, producing Roger at the other end. But what a pitiful version of Roger! His coat was matted and filled with burrs. His head was down and his tail dragged the ground. When Roger allowed his big, fluffy tail to droop, Mrs. Entwhistle knew he was unhappy. It was the tail of woe. He didn't seem to notice Mrs. Entwhistle until she called his name. Then he looked up and burst into a cascade of joyous barks. She hadn't heard Roger bark like that in years. She took a step toward him, but Man-Bun held out a hand.

"Money, then dog," he said.

Mrs. Entwhistle tossed the bag over to him. As his hand closed on it, Pete's voice rang out. "Drop it! Put your hands in the air. You're under arrest."

Man-Bun looked around in surprise, dropping the rope but hanging onto the bag of cash. Roger scurried over to Mrs. Entwhistle as fast as his arthritic legs would carry him. She knelt down and grabbed him into her arms, glad for his slobbery kisses. Then everything seemed to be occurring in slow motion.

Man-Bun turned to run. Pete stepped out from behind a tree and blocked his path, only to be hit in the mid-section by a head-first tackle. She heard the "oof" as Pete's breath left him. Both men went down, the bag burst open, and for a moment it was raining money. Mrs. Entwhistle felt she had plenty of time, in that slow-motion world, to set Roger on the ground, pull out her concealed weapon and walk over to the struggling men. She trained the nozzle of her Mace can directly into Man-Bun's face and let loose, loving the way he screamed and clawed at his eyes. Unfortunately, Pete also got a faceful, but Mrs. Entwhistle subscribed to the philosophy that you can't make an omelet without breaking eggs. She continued to spray until the can was empty.

By then, Pete had rolled out of the line of fire and recovered enough to flip Man-Bun onto his stomach and cuff his hands behind him. He squinted up at Mrs. Entwhistle through tear-streaming eyes. "Good work, Mrs. Entwhistle," he said, between violent coughs. "Now let's pick up your money."

~*~

"Is Roger all right, do you think?" Maxine asked.

He was in his customary spot on the sofa, having devoured a big bowl of dog food, taken several long, splashy drinks of water and endured a warm bath. The little dog was tuckered out, but Mrs. Entwhistle thought that a couple of days of rest would restore him to his usual energy level. He didn't have far to go, after all. Roger wasn't exactly a ball of fire on his best day.

"You know, I think he chased after that big orange tomcat that comes around sometimes," Mrs. Entwhistle said. "He's still a devil when he sees a cat. I bet he went farther than he realized, and then didn't know how to get home. Man-Bun must have seen him on the street and picked him up. Roger'd go to anybody, he doesn't know about stranger-danger. When Man-Bun read Roger's I.D. tag, he got an idea. Not a very good one, as it turned out."

"Well, he's in jail now," Maxine said with

satisfaction, "and I hope he has a good, long stay."

"He's charged with assaulting a federal agent, extortion, theft, cruelty to animals, and I don't know what all, so I think he'll be there awhile."

"Pete saved the day, didn't he?" Maxine said.

"Yes, Pete's a crackerjack," Mrs. Entwhistle agreed. "But Pete and I worked as a team. When he got the wind knocked out of him, it was a good thing I had Mace and knew how to use it."

"Are Pete's eyes all right now?"

"Oh, sure," Mrs. Entwhistle said dismissively, "a little pink yet, and he complains that they itch some, but he'll be fine." She refused to feel guilty about Macing Pete's eyes. She'd only done what had to be done.

Roger's legs paddled and he yipped softly in his sleep. He quieted when Mrs. Entwhistle's hand smoothed his head. The two ladies regarded him with fond smiles.

"Max, I believe I could eat a bowl of that chicken soup now," Mrs. Entwhistle said.

Mrs. Entwhistle Attends Her High School Reunion

"Did you get your invitation?" Maxine asked. She was waving hers in the air.

"Yes, I got it," Mrs. Entwhistle said dismissively. "But I'm not going. It just wouldn't be the same without Floyd."

"Now, Cora, you've been saying that every year since Floyd passed. Let's just go this year. We'll whisper about how old everyone else looks." Maxine's eyes danced with the fun of conspiracy, but Mrs. Entwhistle was unmoved.

"No, I don't think so," she said. "Floyd loved it, and I only went because of him. High school reunions aren't my cup of tea. Just a lot of disappointingly old folks trying to remember their glory days. And the only people who show up are the ones, like us, who stayed in town. You know it'll be the same people we see at the grocery store and church and the library. It might be more interesting if some of those who moved off would come back."

"Well, then!" Maxine said delightedly. "There's no

excuse for you not to go this year, because guess who's going to be there!"

"Who?"

"Giancarlo Cicerino."

Maxine sat back to enjoy the look of amazement on Mrs. Entwhistle's face.

"Really?"

"That's what Mary Sue told me. He's coming all the way from California expressly for this reunion, because it's our sixtieth. Mary Sue said when Giancarlo called her to make his reservation, he said anybody who is still standing is someone he wants to see."

Giancarlo had been the shining star of their high school days. He played football, had his own convertible, was class president, and dated Janine Hasselfress, the prettiest girl in school. Mrs. Entwhistle'd had a secret crush on him for most of senior year, but she'd never breathed a word of it, not even to Maxine. With his smoldering dark Italian eyes and black hair, Giancarlo was out of her league. Besides, she was already going out with Floyd. She suspected Floyd had an inkling of how she felt, though. He'd never liked Giancarlo. Called him Sissy-Pants Cicerino.

"Well. Maybe. It would be fun to see how Giancarlo has aged. Living out there in all that sunshine, he might have the hide of a walrus by now."

"I bet he doesn't," Maxine said dreamily. "I bet he doesn't."

She reached into her capacious bag and pulled out an ancient yearbook. Mrs. Entwhistle couldn't believe Max had not only kept it all these years, but could put her hands on it when she wanted to. Together they scanned the formal black and white graduation photographs of their fellow classmates. Under each picture was a Senior Superlative that supposedly summed up character. Mrs. Entwhistle had been on the yearbook committee and remembered how they'd pondered these descriptors. There was Floyd Entwhistle – Most Industrious; herself, Cora Johnson – Most Determined; Maxine Gober – Best Friend. And Giancarlo Cicerino, smiling confidently into his bright future – Most Likely to Succeed. Privately, Mrs. Entwhistle agreed with Maxine. She bet Giancarlo didn't look like a walrus, either.

~*~

Mrs. Entwhistle hadn't worried about what to wear in a long time. She had her pantsuit, old but still good, that she wore for special occasions, and a couple of nice church dresses. Surveying them in her closet gave her no pleasure. The pantsuit had big shoulder-pads; she was pretty sure they were no longer in style. But if she wore one of the dresses, that meant she'd have to wear pantyhose. Ronnie Sue said nobody but old ladies wore pantyhose anymore. The fact that Mrs. Entwhistle was an old lady did not make her amenable to joining their fashion ranks. She'd noticed that young women just stuffed their naked feet into high heels and went bare-legged. That was all very well if you had smooth, brown legs. Mrs. Entwhistle did not.

"Maxine, I think maybe I'll buy a new outfit," she said one day, trying to sound off-hand. "Not just for the reunion, of course. Something I could wear any time."

"Why, yes, Cora, you should. I saw a beautiful

white pantsuit in Kresyln's window."

"No, I'd look like a nurse in all white. Heaven knows, nurses will probably be needed at our class reunion, but I don't want to be mistaken for one."

"Do you want to go out to the mall? I'll drive, if you want to go."

The mall was a major undertaking for the two ladies. It squatted beside the frightening interstate. Mrs. Entwhistle had given up driving in those snorting, whirling, eddying, horn-blasting, whooshing lanes, but Maxine still ventured forth in her big Lincoln. Mrs. Entwhistle thought Maxine wasn't scared only because she couldn't see or hear very well. She sat so low she had to peek over the top of the steering wheel. Mrs. Entwhistle, taller, saw the near-misses and heard the angry horn-blasts. It was terrifying. But desperate times call for desperate measures.

Mrs. Entwhistle said, "Well, okay, then."

~*~

The ladies emerged from the Lincoln's front seat a little flustered. They fluffed their hair, clutched their purses firmly, took deep breathes and launched themselves into the perfume-scented, Muzak-filled mall. They headed to Macy's, a store with which they were long familiar. But it had been a year since their last visit and everything seemed to have been moved. They wandered for a few minutes, but Mrs. Entwhistle knew they had neither the stamina nor the feet to wander long. She approached a sales clerk at the cosmetics counter, got sprayed with perfume for her trouble, but learned the way to Women's.

Once there, they scanned the racks and racks of

spring clothing. "Everything's sleeveless," Maxine said sadly.

"And short," Mrs. Entwhistle added. "Let's ask where the Alfred Dunner section is."

That was more like it. There were plenty of elastic waistbands and elbow-length sleeves, styles they favored. Mrs. Entwhistle picked out a pantsuit in basic black and held it out for Maxine's inspection. But Max was holding out something herself: a long, periwinkle blue dress. Mrs. Entwhistle shook her head no.

"Oh, try it on, Cora," Maxine said. "This color would be lovely on you."

"But a long dress, Max? I mean, we're just going to be in the school cafeteria."

"You didn't read your invitation very carefully," Maxine said. "The reunion is in the Marriott, the one on the south side of town. It's going to be fancy this year. And besides, long dresses are in style, even for daytime. I'll wear one if you will. Just slip it on. I think it will be perfect for you."

And it was. Mrs. Entwhistle's critical self-assessing eyes raked her image up and down in the full-length, three-way mirror, and she had to admit she looked good. Pretty good. For seventy-eight. Well, that's all you could reasonably expect, right? The long sweep of blue reminded her of how tall and slim she'd been when she was young.

"I'll take it," Mrs. Entwhistle said. "I'll get my hair done at the Curl-E-Cue Corner and wear my pearl earrings." She felt a frisson of excitement.

Shoes. High heels were out of the question. "Don't

need a broken hip," Mrs. Entwhistle said. She tried on a pair of silver slippers. They had absolutely no arch-support and she knew her legs would ache for days after wearing them, but somehow they made her rather large, rather flat feet look smaller. Almost dainty. She bought them. Then she bought a tiny silver beaded purse on a chain.

"Do you think I'd have time to lose a few pounds?" Mrs. Entwhistle had the bit in her teeth now.

"Oh, Cora, why torment yourself?" Maxine said. "You look fine just as you are. Besides, if you lost weight, you'd lose it all in the face. Remember Jenny?"

They had a mutual friend who'd bragged incessantly about losing twenty pounds, seemingly unaware that, as a result, her face had melted into a million wrinkles. The memory made the corners of their mouths turned up just a little bit. Better to keep the plump cheeks, and put up with the other plump parts.

Mrs. Entwhistle declared herself ready. Now she had only to wait. How ridiculous to feel nervous little butterflies in her stomach. For heaven's sake. At her age. And for Sissy-Pants Ciserino. Floyd would have a fit.

~*~

The Marriott's ballroom was too big for their little gathering. Only about fifty people milled around the bar, and maybe half of them were spouses. You could tell the spouses by their bored faces. Nothing worse than somebody else's class reunion, Mrs. Entwhistle thought. She and Floyd had graduated together, so they both knew everyone and shared the memories of high-school high-jinks, so hilarious to those involved, so interminable to those not. You had to feel sorry for the poor husbands and wives of alumni, desperately making small talk and trying to hide glances at their watches.

It would have been impossible to identify the eighteen-year-olds now incarcerated in white heads and stooped bodies had each person not been wearing a name tag containing his or her graduation photo. Could this be bubbly Marilyn Dornan, this frail old lady? And James Keeler, he of the graceful jump shot, walking gingerly on traitorous knees? Frenchy Laurent, drum majorette, holding a cane instead of baton? But somehow, despite the extra pounds and wrinkles, they were laughing and talking, living up to their class motto, "Onward Ever, Backward Never." Mrs. Entwhistle felt a lump in her throat. They were all so brave.

Maxine was getting them both a Diet Coke and Mrs. Entwhistle stood alone by a column entwined with plastic ivy. She knew she must look as antiquated as everyone else, but curled and scented, powdered and lipsticked, wearing the long blue dress and silver slippers, she didn't even feel like herself. She'd worried about carrying her utilitarian black cane with her fancy clothes, but drew the line when Maxine suggested she get a flowered walking stick.

"For heaven's sake," she'd said. "All I need is some slippery new cane so I can fall flat on my face. No, I'll just stick with what I'm used to."

But she did hide it as best she could in the folds of her dress.

There was a stir over by the door. People were looking that way, drifting over, calling to each other. Mrs. Entwhistle looked, too, and saw the entrance of a short,

117

rotund fellow. He was beaming, showing a lot of bright white teeth. His progress was slowed by hand-shaking, back-slapping and hugging, but as he drew nearer, Mrs. Entwhistle saw, with a thrill of recognition, that it was Giancarlo. Suddenly feeling shy, she shrank back behind the column.

Maxine, making her way across the room with a Diet Coke in each hand, was intercepted, thoroughly hugged and kissed on both cheeks by Giancarlo. Blushing a becoming pink, she reached Mrs. Entwhistle slightly out of breath.

"Whooee!" she said. "Here you go. Well, Giancarlo hasn't changed a bit, has he?"

"Was he always that short?" Mrs. Entwhistle said. "I remembered him as being much bigger."

"Well, I expect he's shrunk some," Max said. "But he wasn't ever a real big guy. He just acted like it."

"Is he here alone? No wife?"

"Looks that way. Here he comes now."

"Why, Cora Johnson, I'd know you anywhere!" Giancarlo said, eyeing her name tag as he grabbed Mrs. Entwhistle in a bear hug.

"It's Entwhistle," she gasped. "Oof!"

"Oh, so you married Floyd, then? I used to call him Fuddy-Duddy Floyd," Giancarlo said. "Where that rascal?"

"He had a name for you, too," Mrs. Entwhistle said in an icy voice. Nobody, not even Giancarlo Cicerino, disparaged Floyd in her presence. "He passed several years ago."

"Oh, sorry to hear that. Great guy, great guy," Giancarlo said. "Let's sit together at dinner. We've got a lot to catch up on, am I right?"

Mrs. Entwhistle felt flattered in spite of herself, but the effect was somewhat spoiled when he turned and said exactly the same thing to Maxine. He offered each of them an arm, and escorted them to seats at one of the round tables.

"So!" Giancarlo said, beaming to his left and to his right. "How are you girls doing? Maxine, can you still fit into your cheerleader's outfit? And Cora, are you still the smartest girl in the room?"

"Well, I shouldn't think so," Mrs. Entwhistle said. "I've lived long enough to know how much I don't know. Besides, I've been in a lot of rooms since high school, haven't you?"

"Oh, yes, yes, indeed," said Giancarlo. If he'd had a mustache, he'd have twirled it. "Lived in California all these years, cradle of the movie industry, you know. My second wife, ex-wife, that is, was an actress. You may have heard of her – Myra McDonald?"

Mrs. Entwhistle and Maxine smiled and shook their heads.

"Well, she wasn't exactly famous, but she was in the industry and we got to know a lot of people. That's what we call the movie business – the industry," he explained.

"What was your work?" Mrs. Entwhistle asked.

"I was in promotion, marketing, development, you know, ideas…" Giancarlo said, waving his hand vaguely. "I was an idea man."

"What exactly does an idea man do?" Mrs. Entwhistle wondered.

"We think up work for other people to do!" Giancarlo said, with a wink and a laugh. "Actually, I'm still at it."

Mrs. Entwhistle thought of the years in which Floyd rose at six a.m., made a pot of coffee and brought her a cup, then set off for a full day's work at the airplane factory. When he retired, he got a plaque and a camera to take pictures of all the trips they never had time to take before he died. Floyd didn't expect other people to do work he thought up for them. He did it himself.

Giancarlo had a lot to say about famous people he'd met, done business with, dated or married. There seemed to be quite a few on all fronts. Mrs. Entwhistle counted four ex-wives and marveled at the energy – and money - it must have taken to get in and out of all those relationships. Giancarlo was still talking.

Her thoughts strayed. Had she remembered to take out a carton of orange juice to thaw for tomorrow's breakfast? Maybe she and Max could stop at the bakery on the way home and get some of those good cinnamon rolls. Was the bakery open late?

"Now, remember, when the band starts playing, save the first dance for me," Giancarlo said, looking deep into Mrs. Entwhistle's eyes.

She couldn't think if she'd cleaned her trifocals before leaving home. These new non-reflective lenses attracted dirt and smears like twin magnets. Mrs. Entwhistle thought smugly that she hadn't needed cataract surgery yet. Had her mind always wandered like this, or did it only happen when she was bored?

Giancarlo cleared his throat importantly, signaling that he was about to say something significant. "I'm just wondering: do you ladies both own your own homes?"

"Why, yes, we do," Maxine answered. "We often say it's a shame we don't just share a place instead of maintaining two houses, but we're both attached to our homes and set in our ways, I guess."

"That's great, that's wonderful. And I bet both those houses are long paid for, am I right?"

They nodded, exchanging puzzled glances.

"Now here's what I want to talk to you about. Do you have any idea how much equity you're sitting on? Why, thousands and thousands of dollars! Did you know that you can get a reverse mortgage on your homes and free up a lot of extra spending money? Why should all that cash be tied up in your houses when you could use it to travel, or do some home repairs you've been putting off? Get a new car, maybe. And you'd never have to pay it back. How does that sound? Most of us could use some extra moolah, am I right?" Giancarlo smiled widely, his too-white teeth seeming to Mrs. Entwhistle like predatory fangs. "I can hook you up with a reputable finance company. You know me, you can trust me, and I'd be your agent, look out for your best interests and all that. What have you got to lose, am I right?"

"Well, your fee, for one thing. My house will be about all I have to leave my children," Mrs. Entwhistle said. "If I borrow against it, won't they have to pay it back when I'm gone?"

"Sure, sure, or let the house go back to the

mortgage company. But what do you care? You won't be around to see it. We'll get you a bumper sticker for your new car that says, 'I'm spending my children's inheritance.' You don't owe your kids a dime, not a dime. Live it up while you're alive, that's what I always say. Am I right?"

"No, you're not right, and that's not what I always say," Mrs. Entwhistle said. She felt a flush of rage at Giancarlo for daring to slight her children, if only in theory. Her voice rose so that several people at nearby tables glanced at her. "I always say, don't take advantage of old friendships to try to sell something. That's what I always say."

Giancarlo's affable smile fled. "Well!" he said huffily, "I was just trying to help some old friends - senior citizens."

"We're all the same age," Maxine reminded him. "Same class, remember? And I don't want a reverse mortgage, either."

"Excuse me, ladies." Giancarlo rose with wounded dignity, crossed the room and approached another group. Maxine and Mrs. Entwhistle heard him say, "Good evening, good evening. How are you lovely ladies tonight? I'll bet every one of you comes from a beautiful home, am I right?"

"For heaven's sake," Mrs. Entwhistle said, shaking her head. "You just never know how people will turn out, do you?"

"Are you okay? Do you want to go home?" Maxine asked.

Mrs. Entwhistle suspected that Maxine knew about

her secret crush, but she'd never, by hint, nudge or wink, reveal that she knew. Mrs.Entwhistle thought for the thousandth time that there couldn't be a better friend than Maxine.

"Go home? Not on your life," Mrs. Entwhistle said. "We haven't had dinner yet, and I'm hungry. Plus, I want to hear the class roll called so we can find out what happened to everybody and who-all is already dead."

"We know what happened to Giancarlo," Maxine said.

"We sure do. I just wonder how he got his teeth so white."

"Maybe by chewing up widows and orphans," Maxine suggested. They laughed in perfect harmony, as only old friends can laugh.

"I'm still glad I bought this dress, though," Mrs. Entwhistle said. "I might wear it again, who knows? It never hurts to look one's best. Am I right?"

Mrs. Entwhistle Cancels Christmas

Cora Entwhistle had mixed emotions. The thing was, she didn't believe the Christmas story, but a respectable elderly lady living in a small town couldn't voice such doubts. In her opinion, a virginal conception announced by angels was highly suspect. Why not just admit Mary was expecting before she got married? That was a story old as humans. As for the whole manger/shepherds/wise men meme, she couldn't buy it. The unassailable fact of the matter was that a person who'd lived hundreds of years ago was still so influential that time was dated from his birth. That seemed significant enough without all the attendant window-dressing. But she kept such views to herself. After all, Winter Solstice had been celebrated from time immemorial; it just came wrapped in red and green these days.

Some things about the holiday she liked: midnight service on Christmas Eve, when the familiar old church took on an air of mystery and strangeness; the table groaning under the feast of favorite foods; seeing her children and grandchildren all together. Some things she disliked: all that cooking, the difficulty of finding a date to gather family, the mad orgy of shopping and wrapping presents, the tension of deadlines and budget versus list. But she'd learned to concentrate on what she liked and ignore the rest as much as possible.

Mrs. Entwhistle was not one who did her Christmas shopping in July. She believed the holiday season had already overlapped its boundaries like a fat man in an airplane seat. She refused to think about it until December first. That was still plenty of time if you didn't plan to go mad and make a big fuss over everything. In due time, she called her daughter, Diane.

"Hello, Mama," her daughter said.

"How did you know it was me?" Mrs. Entwhistle demanded

"You always ask that. I have Caller I.D., remember?"

"Oh, yes. It's spooky, though, like you can see through the telephone."

"Yes, Mama. How are you today?"

"Oh, fine, honey, just fine. Listen, I'm calling about Christmas. When's a good day for me to have everyone here?"

"Well, let me just look at my calendar. It's already filled up; seems to do that earlier every year. Let's see. We have John's family coming on the Sunday before. And the kids are in the church program on Christmas Eve. And on Christmas Day, we want to stay home so they can play with their new toys. The week-end after, we're taking them to Dollywood. It's their big present this year."

"Any week-days available?" Mrs. Entwhistle asked, through gritted teeth.

"John has to work every day except Christmas."

"I see."

"Sorry, Mama, I don't mean to be uncooperative, it's just such a busy time with the kids and two sets of families to celebrate with. And you've left it kind of late."

"Today is December second. I wouldn't call that late."

"Why don't you just come here, Mama? You could come over on Christmas Eve, spend the night and watch the children open their presents in the morning."

Mrs. Entwhistle shuddered at the mental image of two over-excited grandchildren ripping and shrieking their way through the ridiculous pile of presents that she knew lay under the tree at her daughter's house. She pictured the mounds of wrapping paper and empty boxes, the hectic red cheeks of children who didn't know whether to laugh or cry, and so did both. She envisioned the spilled cocoa sticky on the floor; the quarrelling over who got more or better presents; the exhausted faces of parents trying, against all common sense, to enjoy the occasion. No, thanks. Not even if they were her own children and grandchildren. She had an ace up her sleeve for just such an occasion.

"What about Roger?" she asked.

"Mama, you know Roger can't come. Jeannie's allergic; she'd spend the whole holiday sniffling and coughing."

"Well, I can't just leave him at home."

Mrs. Entwhistle's little dog was her built-in excuse when she didn't want to do something. Nobody much wanted Roger to visit, not that it was his fault that he had those skin problems and a bit of an odor. He was old, after all. And he did get confused sometimes when he was away from home, and forget to go to the door when he wanted out. That one time he'd lifted his leg on Diane's new sofa, Mrs. Entwhistle had never heard such a scream. Scared the poor little dog so much he dried up in mid-stream. It was not lost on Mrs. Entwhistle that Jeannie's allergy developed right after that visit.

"All right, Diane," she said into the phone now. "Let me check with Tommy. You be thinking if there is some time you might squeeze your mother into your schedule."

Mrs. Entwhistle hung up, hearing Diane's sputtering as she replaced the handset of her old-fashioned desk model telephone. She dialed Tommy's number at the office.

"Accounting," he said crisply.

"Tommy, it's Mama."

"Oh, hi, Mama," Tommy said, his tone changing instantly from business-crisp to whiney-casual. "I'm being rushed off my feet right now, could I call you back later?"

"This won't take a minute. I'm just trying to see when you can come for Christmas."

"I'm not celebrating Christmas this year," Tommy said. "Since Judy took the girls and left me, I don't have anything to celebrate. In fact, I'm going to ignore the whole deal. Maybe go skiing."

"You don't ski, Tommy," Mrs. Entwhistle said.

"I might learn."

"I see. All right, then. 'Bye."

Mrs. Entwhistle was darned if she was going to spend one more minute begging her children to fit her into their plans. She sat staring out the window at the bird feeder. The black-capped chickadees and sober gray sparrows were having a grand time kicking the expensive sun flower seeds to the ground, where a couple of gluttonous squirrels Hoovered them up. Apparently *they* have time to get together, Mrs. Entwhistle thought. Then she rose decisively.

"Come on, Roger," she said, rattling his leash and harness. The little dog walked stiffly over and extended his neck toward the harness. She slipped it over his head, buckled it around his belly, got into her coat, warm hat and gloves, and they set out for their daily walk. Walking was a good time to think, and she had some thinking to do.

"Well, who says Christmas has to be celebrated, anyway?" she said to herself. Mrs. Entwhistle often talked aloud as she walked. Let people think she had one of those cell phone thingies clipped on her ear. Half the population could be seen talking into thin air these days, like crazy people escaped from the Home.

"I'll just do something else this year, on my own. Maybe I'll volunteer to serve the Christmas meal at the homeless shelter. I can plop turkey and dressing onto a paper plate as well as anyone. That'd show Diane and Tommy."

Of course, Diane and Tommy had a fit when she

told them. They felt guilty, as Mrs. Entwhistle knew they would.

"I'm not mad at you," she explained several times. "You are both busy. Fine. I can fill my time quite nicely, thank you. You're off the hook, because Christmas with me is officially cancelled. I'll see you after the holidays, when things settle down."

And that was that.

~*~

They were glad to have her, at the homeless shelter. "We always need volunteers," said the perky lady who took Mrs. Entwhistle's call. "We start prepping the night before, get those big turkeys into the oven at midnight, carve early in the morning, everything goes in the warming oven, and then we begin serving our clients at eleven. People come through until around three, and then we clean up and go home. Can you come for the whole day?"

"No, dear, I'm seventy-eight years of age." Mrs. Entwhistle didn't hesitate to play the age card when it suited her. "I'll come at ten-thirty and stand in the serving line. As long as my old legs will allow," she added, prudently giving herself an out in case she needed it. Advanced age should have some compensation to balance out the things you lost, she figured. Heaven knew there were enough of those.

At the appointed time, she drove into the mission's parking lot. Spaces were scarce. You'd think the homeless people wouldn't be driving, she reflected, maneuvering gingerly into a too-small spot. The person on her right would not be able to get their driver's side door open, but it was the best she could do. Maybe she'd leave before that person did.

Entering the warm, brightly lit kitchen, she felt shy. She knew no one, and that in itself was a novelty. Having lived in her house for fifty years, her neighborhood and its inhabitants were as familiar as her own face in the mirror. A smiling, hurrying woman in a big apron came forward, holding out her hand.

"Hi! I'm Marge!" she shouted.

"Cora Entwhistle. I called…"

"Yes! I was expecting you! Come on in and get your apron!"

Mrs. Entwhistle mentally christened her Shouter. Obediently, she slipped the stained white apron over her head and tied the strings in a firm bow behind her back.

"People! People! Our clients are waiting at the door already! I need someone to go out and tell them to line up in an orderly way! Mrs. Entwhistle, would you do that?"

Mrs. Entwhistle nodded and moved toward the glass double doors, beyond which could be seen a jostling throng. Everyone seemed to be dressed alike, in dark jackets, black knitted caps and camo pants. They looked cold. And menacing.

She pushed the door open, stepped outside and heard the lock click as the door shut behind her. Great, now she was locked out in the cold without a coat, in the middle of a mob of hungry strangers. Sure to get pneumonia, if not get shot.

"Uh, folks…friends," she said in her naturally-carrying voice, "I've been asked to tell you to form an orderly line before the doors are unlocked."

"I was in an orderly line, until this shit-head pushed in front of me," said one woman. She cast a baleful look at the offender.

"She left and then came back and jumped the line," he said. "If you leave, you give up your place, right?"

"Now, now, 'tis the season," Mrs. Entwhistle said, but she was met by stony stares. "You know, to be jolly," she explained.

"Ain't nothin' jolly about standin' out here in th' cold," someone muttered.

"If you're too good to wait, why don't you get on outta here?" said an anonymous voice in the crowd.

"Don't you tell me what to do; I'll break your sorry head."

Mrs. Entwhistle wondered how the newspaper headlines would read in tomorrow's paper: *Elderly Woman Killed in Riot at Homeless Shelter*. Or, best case scenario: *Saintly Volunteer Quells Homeless Unrest*. "I certainly wouldn't call myself a hero," she rehearsed in her mind. "I just did what anyone.,.."

At that moment, Shouter swung the glass doors open wide and Mrs. Entwhistle surfed into the warm dining room on a tide of humanity. She washed up near the kitchen door and took her place in the serving line. The plates started coming. Plop, shuffle, plop, shuffle, it was endless.

"Make eye contact! Say Merry Christmas!" Shouter shouted. But Mrs. Entwhistle barely had time to glance up from the enormous vat of dressing.

She remembered the old *I Love Lucy* episode in which Lucy and Ethel worked on the candy factory assembly line, and, unable to keep up with the conveyor belt, stuffed chocolates into their mouths and clothing. At least dressing would be warm next to the skin, if it came to that.

Finally the line slowed and then trickled out. The volunteers were encouraged to fix themselves plates and Mrs. Entwhistle did so, having worked up a good appetite. Like the clients, this would be her only Christmas dinner. She looked around for a congenial table.

"Mind if I join you?" she asked, approaching three seated women.

"Sit down, dearie, take a load off," one of the woman said. "I'm Rachel, this here is Patricia, and that's Mary."

"Cora," Mrs. Entwhistle said, dropping heavily into the folding chair.

"Tired you out, didn't we? You have yourself some turkey now and catch your second wind."

The women continued the conversation that Mrs. Entwhistle's arrival had interrupted. "You need to leave now if you're gonna walk to the women's shelter in time to get a bed," Rachel said. "I'm gonna sleep in my place. I've got a little pup tent up in those woods off the interstate. Got me a propane heater, so I'll be okay."

"Willy caught hisself on fire with one of them heaters," Patricia said.

"Yeah, but Willy's an idiot. Probably had all kinds of blankets and papers piled right up on it."

Mrs. Entwhistle thought of her own bed, never before viewed as luxurious, and of the hot bath she intended to sink into when she got home. The women had draped their outerwear over the backs of their chairs - second-hand woolen coats that had seen better days, cleared from closets of plenty. The requisite knitted caps were still on their heads, no doubt to hide hair that wouldn't stand the light of day. Fingerless gloves and one pair of mittens knitted in a reindeer pattern lay on the table. Were they warm enough on this glitteringly cold day? And what about the nights? Where were these women's families?

Mrs. Entwhistle spoke up. "Do you have children? Have you seen them over Christmas?"

All six eyes turned to her. They regarded her silently for a long moment.

Rachel spoke first. "My boys are in California, I reckon. That's what they said when they left a couple years ago. I heard from one of them for a while, but when I had to give up the house, I didn't have no address to give him. I had a cell phone 'till someone stole it off me while I was sleepin'. I don't guess my boys would know where to find me if they was lookin'."

"I never had kids," Patricia said. "Never been married. When the factory closed, I couldn't make my rent no more, so I had to get out on the street. Been out there for three years now, and it ain't so bad, once you figure out where to get help when you need it."

Mary's head was down. Tears leaked slowly from her closed eyes and made tracks down her cheeks. She said nothing. Mrs. Entwhistle drew in her breath to speak, but Patricia caught her eye. No, her head shook, and she placed a finger on her lips. Mrs. Entwhistle exhaled and closed her mouth. She understood. Some things went too deep for words.

"So!" Patricia said, with forced cheer, "The women's shelter is real fine. We c'n take showers and wash our clothes and on Saturdays there's a gal comes and gives haircuts. Lotta times someone brings in a big pot of soup. But..." she hesitated. "Well, it's a mite far from here. If you was to give us a ride, that would sure be a help. If it wouldn't be too much trouble."

Mrs. Entwhistle's glance fell on Mary's foot, clad in a filthy orthopedic walking boot and elevated on another folding chair. "How did you hurt your foot?" she asked.

"Oh, just got a dang infection between my toes. Feet are wet a lot. It's getting better, but it still hurts like hell when I walk on it."

"Of course, I'll drive you to the shelter," Mrs. Entwhistle said with some difficulty. There seemed to be a big lump in her throat. "Whenever you're ready."

Coats and gloves were donned, with much winding of scarves around necks. They need waterproof boots, Mrs. Entwhistle thought, resolving to go to Wal-Mart the next morning and purchase several pair. And maybe some warm flannel shirts, too.

Rachel said good-bye in the parking lot and set off on foot for her pup tent in the woods. She turned and waved several times before she disappeared into the trees. The other women climbed into Mrs. Entwhistle's car. Never had her old Buick been so appreciated. Patricia and Mary commented on how nice and clean Mrs. Entwhistle kept it. They complimented her on the soft seats and strong heater and smooth ride. When they arrived at the women's shelter, both women gripped her hands, told her she was as good as an angel, and wished her a Merry Christmas as they hauled themselves back out into the frigid and darkening day.

"Merry Christmas," Mrs. Entwhistle said back. She'd slipped a twenty dollar bill into Mary's coat pocket. A little voice whispered in her head: she'll probably buy a bottle with it. I don't care, Mrs. Entwhistle answered. Whatever gives her a little comfort.

She resolved to go back to the shelter in the morning with the contents of the crowded coat closet in her front hall. After all, I can only wear one coat at a time, she thought. Any more just get in the way.

Driving home in the gathering dusk, she silenced the radio and told herself a story instead. "Joseph had to register with the census so he could be taxed. That's the most believable part of the whole thing. We can all relate to that. And anybody who's had a baby knows they come when they darn well please, so Mary could have been caught by surprise with those first labor pains. Maybe the shepherds really did leave their flocks and walk a ways to see the new baby, just for something to break the monotony of sitting in the fields looking at sheep all day and night. A new baby is always interesting. Now, the three wise men – no way they'd have shown up that night, all the way from Asia or China or wherever it was. But I guess there could have been rumors that got them curious, too. Maybe they were heading that way anyway, and decided to stop in and see for themselves. It was different back in those days; folks didn't get their news on the television or the Internet. Stories probably got better as they were passed along, like a big game of Gossip.

135

Could have been some bright stars in the sky, too. No city lights to drown them out. But angels, now—there I have to draw the line."

It was almost dark now, but home was near. She pictured Roger, waiting by the door to greet her exuberantly. Maybe she'd build a fire in the fireplace, take a long, hot bath, have a cup of soup, and call the kids to wish them a Merry Christmas. Her children may have been unavailable today, but they were there for her at the other end of the telephone line. They knew where to find her. They'd always know that.

Filled, suddenly, with contentment, Mrs. Entwhistle hummed a little. Then she sang the words, turning her face up to the first bright evening star, her quavery voice cracking on the high notes: "The first Noel, the angels did say, was to certain poor shepherds, in fields as they lay."

It didn't seem to matter anymore whether the Christmas story was true in a literal sense. There was a kernel of truth in there somewhere, and it was enough.

Mrs. Entwhistle Aces a Lab Test

"Oh, for heaven's sake, let him out," Mrs. Entwhistle said to her hostess, Pearl Entwhistle.

Pearl was her sister-in-law - Floyd's baby sister, as he referred to her until his dying day. Well, actually, within the family she was never called anything but Baby Pea, supposedly Floyd's early effort to say her name. But Mrs. Entwhistle simply could not utter it. Baby Pea, for a woman in her seventies? Baby Pea, for a woman of considerable bulk, whose only claim to infancy was her proclivity for weeping during Hallmark commercials? No, there was no way that name would ever pass her lips.

Now, Mrs. Entwhistle was having lunch with Pearl, something the ladies did as infrequently as possible. They kept up a relationship out of respect for Floyd's memory. Other than that, they had little in common. Despite more than fifty years of familial ties, Cora and Pearl Entwhistle maintained a certain formality with one another.

They were seated in Pearl's pink dining room,

dipping their spoons daintily into a cold consommé Pearl considered a hearty lunch. Mrs. Entwhistle thought longingly of the leftover beef stew residing in her refrigerator at home. Oh, well, she'd have it for dinner. Early dinner.

The captive in question, howling for freedom, was Pearl's big, black Labrador retriever, Zeus. Like many Labradors, Zeus never left puppyhood behind. He loved to romp and run in crazy circles, splash in any available body of water, and then shake himself like a whirling dervish, soaking everything within a wide radius.

That Pearl should have a dog like Zeus boggled Mrs. Entwhistle's mind. Pearl, with her sequined toilet tissue covers, her lace curtains, her floral dresses. If ever anyone was a "poodle person," it would be Pearl. And yet there was Zeus, throwing himself against the basement door, baying broken-heartedly at such volume that conversation had to be suspended.

"He might as well sniff me and get it over with," Mrs. Entwhistle said resignedly. "That dog can't stand not to be in the middle of things."

"I'll just get him, then, if you're sure you don't mind," Pearl said, heading for the door with fussy little steps. She opened it with a smile of delight, unleashing eighty pounds of muscles and energy. Zeus exploded into the dining room and crashed into Mrs. Entwhistle's chair, knocking it several inches off center.

"Zeus! Bad doggie," Pearl cooed. "Sit! Sit!"

Ignoring Zeus's disinclination to do so, Pearl sat down herself, shook out her napkin and picked up her soup spoon, as oblivious as if the Hound of the

Baskervilles lived at some other address. Mrs. Entwhistle's napkin went sailing, victim of an enthusiastic paw. Her consommé sloshed out of the bowl as Zeus put his saucer-sized front feet on the table to check out the menu. Doggie kisses fogged her eyeglasses and her lap was thoroughly sniffed.

"Now, then, Zeus," she said, with all the firmness she could muster. "That's enough. Sit."

Zeus's rear end hit the floor as he looked up at her with a grin. He recognized an Alpha human when he saw one, but he couldn't help that his tail revolved like the rotor of a helicopter, propelling him once again into action. Mrs. Entwhistle endured Zeus's spade-shaped head pushing up under her arm. She tolerated his furry weight when he sat on her feet and leaned on her legs. Finally, momentarily tired out by his own exuberance, Zeus stretched out on his side with a long groan and went to sleep.

Mrs. Entwhistle thought of Roger, also asleep, at home. The little dog would be on his favorite couch cushion, snoring lightly, keeping one ear cocked for her return. Roger wasn't perfect, but his faults could be attributed to his advanced years. A certain amount of forgivable flatulence. A tendency to carry food to various parts of the house and forget about it. A proclivity to dribble when he got excited. Mrs. Entwhistle could live with it. But how Pearl lived with this monster – unimaginable.

Pearl stepped in from the kitchen with dessert: her signature lemon bars and Earl Grey tea in a blue china pot. She was famous for those lemon bars, and Mrs. Entwhistle perked up. Conversation flowed more easily, primed by sugar and relief that lunch was almost over.

Mrs. Entwhistle felt Zeus stir at her feet, but for once the dog left her alone. Her attention was firmly fixed on the lemon bars, anyway. Just as she accepted her third, she saw out of the corner of her eye that Zeus was walking around the dining room with a handbag dangling from his neck. Her handbag.

She'd made that bag herself, out of scraps from her old dresses and Floyd's shirts, and even some of the kids' clothes. She'd pieced and quilted and sewn that bag, and felt proud of its uniqueness. It was not meant to be soaked in dog slobber. Zeus wore a bemused expression, but he was nothing if not a good sport. Since he found himself somehow in possession of a purse – well, he'd just make the best of it. His life, after all, was full of inexplicable surprises.

The ladies' eyes met across the table, Pearl's wide with apprehension. They turned their gazes to Zeus, who wagged his tail vigorously, sweeping a small scatter rug into the next room. He looked hopefully from one face to the other, his teeth bared in a doggy smile, then bowed over his front legs in the classic canine invitation to play. Mrs. Entwhistle felt an irresistible hilarity set up housekeeping in her soul. She grinned. She guffawed. She howled. She leaned her face on her hands and laughed until tears of mirth fell on Pearl's white tablecloth.

Zeus, delighted to be the focus of such goodwill, capered around the room tossing his head. Small objects were flung forth from the bag, orbiting the big dog like satellites – Mrs. Entwhistle's lipstick, her coin purse, her address book, her ballpoint pen.

"I'm so sorry, Cora," Pearl said, light winking off her

diamond rings as her hands fluttered in the air. "Zeus! Bad dog! Come here!"

Predictably, Zeus continued his happy dance. Mrs. Entwhistle finally lifted her head, wiped her eyes on her napkin, and regained her composure except for a few stray giggles. Zeus came to sit at her feet, gazing up into her eyes. She slipped the purse strap over his head and restored her scattered possessions.

"Oh, my," she said. "A laugh like that - you couldn't buy it with cash money."

"You're not mad, Cora?" Pearl asked, anxiety clouding her face. "Zeus didn't mean any harm."

"No, I'm not mad. In fact, I don't remember when I've had such a good time. It's a day to remember, Baby Pea."

Mrs. Entwhistle Gets Stuck in an Elevator

Mrs. Entwhistle regarded the people in the elevator when the door opened. There were six already in there. Well, it was roomy enough; six wasn't so bad. She hated to be crammed into a small space with strangers, but six would be okay. She entered and turned around to face the doors as they swooshed shut just inches from her face. She pushed the button for the fifth floor. Then, along with her fellow passengers, she centered herself in an island of private space.

They ascended with a jerk. Ping, second floor. Ping, third floor. Ping, fourth floor. Just as Mrs. Entwhistle was gathering herself to disembark at the sound of the next ping, the elevator stopped, shuddering at its own disobedience. The passengers stirred, looked at each other, looked at the control panel, and saw the floor indicator was blank.

"Push five," advised a voice from the rear.

Mrs. Entwhistle reached over and pushed five. Nothing happened. She pushed again. Nothing.

"Here, let me try it," said the owner of the voice, a large man in an expensive suit.

Like his finger has magic powers, Mrs. Entwhistle thought, but she made room for him. His large, masculine digit had no better results than hers. Hah! She thought. But then she realized they were well and truly stuck between floors, and it wasn't funny. Immediately, although the thought hadn't crossed her mind before, she wished she could go to the bathroom.

Mrs. Entwhistle glanced at the people around her. Everyone looked tense and frightened as they thumbed their cell phones. Blocked by the concrete elevator shaft, no signals made it in or out. The large man was frowning magisterially, as though he could command the elevator to move by the sheer force of his importance. A tired-looking mother was whispering to her little girl, who looked to be about six. Mrs. Entwhistle noticed she was missing both her front teeth. It reminded her of Diane at that age, when her gap-toothed smile was especially sweet. There was a young man wearing black leather. Probably belonged to the big Harley-Davison taking up a prime parking space in front of the building. He was trying to appear blasé, but his eyes betrayed him, darting from face to face. At the very back stood a middle-aged couple holding hands. Mrs. Entwhistle knew immediately they were not married. Aside from the public hand-holding, there was an aura of musky young love about them that didn't match their ages. These were her fellow prisoners.

"Try going down," Black Leather said briefly.

The elevator remained stubbornly immobile.

"Try the phone."

But the phone seemed to be dead.

"Push the emergency button."

This was more promising. They could hear a distant ringing. Surely, someone else in the building would hear it, too.

Mrs. Entwhistle wondered what brought them all to the courthouse that day. She was there to file an appeal of her most recent homeowner's tax assessment.

"It's not that I mind paying my fair share of taxes," she'd said to Maxine. "But my assessment jumped 45% in one year. Now, you know that can't be right. No way I could sell this house and get what they say it's worth. Not that I would sell, anyway."

Maxine nodded. "Mine went up, too, but not by that much," she said. "I guess I'll just let it ride. It won't cost me that much more in taxes."

"My taxes will go up considerably," Mrs. Entwhistle said grimly. She was careful about expenses. "Floyd would march right down to the courthouse and demand that someone explain to him exactly how they came up with such a figure. That's what I should do, too, and you know, I think I will."

So here she was, on a hot summer Tuesday morning, trapped like a rat in a metal box going nowhere. She fought down a flutter of panic. To distract herself, she spoke.

"I'm Cora Entwhistle," she said. Her voice sounded loud to her own ears. She made an effort to tone it down. "I'm just on my way to the Tax Office."

"Judge Harrison Abernathy," the large man said.

His smile was charming. It made him look twenty years younger. "I work here in the courtroom on the seventh floor. I think my docket will be starting a little late today."

"Mama, how long do we have to be in here?" the little girl said. "I'm thirsty."

"Here you go, sweetie," said the middle-aged woman, disengaging her hand from her partner's long enough to pull a bottle of water from her handbag.

"Uh, thanks, but just a sip, Cathy," her mother said. "Bathroom," she mouthed to the woman, who mouthed back, "Oops!" Cathy upended the bottle before her mother could stop her.

"Let's all get acquainted, since we might be here for a few minutes," Judge Abernathy said. "You know me and Mrs. Entwhistle, and now we know Cathy." He smiled warmly at the little girl, and she smiled back.

"I'm Julia Roberts, not-the-actress," said her mother, with the air of someone who's heard all the jokes just about twice too often.

"Yo, Bruce Feathers," said Black Leather, then jutted out his jaw and dared anyone to laugh.

"We're on our way to get married," the middle-aged man said. "In another half-hour, we'll be Allie and Lawrence Landerfelt. That is, if we get out of here by then."

"Why, I believe you're coming to see me," Judge Abernathy said. "I remember seeing your name on today's schedule, Mr. Landerfelt. I'm the judge who's scheduled to perform your wedding ceremony."

Hands were shaken all around. Then there seemed

to be nothing else to say. Bruce Feathers was sweating profusely. Perspiration dripped off his nose and he swiped it away with the back of his hand.

"Are you okay, young man?" Mrs. Entwhistle asked.

"Just…I get claustrophobia," Bruce said. He looked around desperately. "I gotta get outa here!"

He jostled Mrs. Entwhistle aside and began pounding on the door. "Help! Help!" he screamed. Little Cathy looked on with enormous eyes and a trembling bottom lip. This would never do.

"Stop it at once," Mrs. Entwhistle said. She spoke with no particular emphasis but she made eye contact. Mrs. Entwhistle's eye contact could be formidable.

Bruce lowered his arms and his head. "Sit down," Mrs. Entwhistle directed. "Right on the floor. Take off that hot jacket." She reached in her purse, pulled out the envelope holding her tax papers and fanned Bruce with it. "Now take deep breaths. You're okay. We're just a bit inconvenienced, that's all. We'll have a story to tell our families this evening."

Julia Roberts chose that moment to swoon. Mrs. Entwhistle hadn't seen anyone swoon in many years. It was different than fainting. Fainters tend to go down like felled trees. Swooners sag at the knees. Their eyes roll up and their faces turn an unusual color. All this, Julia demonstrated. Judge Abernathy caught her as she slid gently down the wall.

"Here," Allie said, handing over another water bottle. The woman was a walking hydration station. "Splash a little water in her face."

"Mama gets this way sometimes," Cathy said calmly. She patted her mother's cheeks. "Wake up, Mama," she called.

Julia's eyes fluttered open, vacant only as long as it took to register that she was the focus of six alarmed faces.

"Oh, goodness, I'm sorry. I didn't eat anything this morning, that's why. And it's so warm in here."

Bruce reached in the pocket of his leather jacket and offered a linty piece of beef jerky. "Protein," he said.

Mrs. Entwhistle nodded at him approvingly. Julia looked at the offering with narrowed eyes, but she broke off a piece, wiped it on her skirt, and began chewing.

"Better now, ma'am?" Judge Abernathy asked Julia. When she nodded, he said, "Then let's continue getting to know each other. As I already told you I'm a judge here in the court house. I'm semi-retired, so I fill in where needed. Today, I'm hearing traffic cases and misdemeanors. And marrying these nice people, of course."

Lawrence Landerfelt beamed. "Allie and I have been together for ten years," he said. "We just got up this morning and decided today's the day to make it legal."

Allie's face creased with worry. "I don't know, though, Larry. Maybe being stuck in this elevator is a bad omen. Maybe we should find a more auspicious day."

"Oh, c'mon, Allie. You know what I think of your superstitious nonsense."

"Yes? Well, who was right when I said we shouldn't go to the mountains, I just had a feeling, and then we had a flat tire on that narrow, winding road? And who was right when I said maybe we'd better not eat at the Korean barbeque, and you ended up in the emergency room? And who was right…"

Lawrence interrupted. "Okay, but those things could have been predicted by just using common sense. It doesn't take a clairvoyant to figure out bald tires might go flat, and the beef tasted funny."

"Well, whether it's common sense or clairvoyance, I seem to have more of it than you," Allie said, putting as much distance between herself and Lawrence as was possible in the crowded space.

Lawrence looked glumly down at the floor. Mrs. Entwhistle stepped into the awkward moment.

"I've lived in this town all my life. My husband, Floyd, passed away some years ago. I have two children, Diane and Tom, who think I'm hardly capable of tying my shoes. Now you," she said to Bruce, who was looking panicky again.

"Bruce Feathers, like I said. I ride a Harley and work in a garage where we fix 'em. I'm here because I got a ticket for violating the noise ordinance. Who the hell knew there was one? I was just heading home after the bar closed and this two-bit cop pulled me over and said my bike was too loud for that time of night. Gave me a ticket that'll cost me $110. It ain't fair, and I'm gonna tell the damn judge…"

Bruce broke off, the awful realization dawning in his face that he'd indeed just told the damn judge. "Jesus," he muttered. "Could this day get any worse?"

"Mama!" Cathy said. "I gotta go to the bathroom. I

gotta go bad!"

"You'll just have to hold it, honey," Julia said. "We can't get to a bathroom right now."

"I caaaaan't," Cathy wailed. And she couldn't. The smell of urine permeated the air.

Mrs. Entwhistle smiled at the distressed little girl. "There," she said, "you feel better now, don't you? Don't worry, it can happen to anybody, even grown-ups." Her own bladder gave a sympathetic pang. "Now, tell us what grade you're in. I bet you're in third."

"No," Cathy said, giggling. "I'm in first grade. And see, I losted two tooths. The Tooth Fairy left me a dollar under my pillow."

"Why, for heaven's sake," Mrs. Entwhistle said, "I thought you were much older. You got a whole dollar for your tooth. Did you spend it?"

Cathy's recitation of the purchases made with her dollar took her mind off her wet underpants. Julia shot a grateful look at Mrs. Entwhistle.

"And what about you, Mrs. Roberts?" Judge Abernathy asked.

"Oh, I'm just a housewife. I mean, I have been up to now, but today I'm applying for a job in the County Clerk's office. Since my husband went...well, I need to work now. My mom was going to keep Cathy, but she got a migraine. If I'm late for my interview, that's a black mark right off the bat. Then I show up with my child in tow, which I know is unprofessional."

"Don't you worry about any of that. It can't be helped, and I'll vouch for you," the judge said.

"I'll stay with Cathy while you have your interview," Mrs. Entwhistle said, surprising herself. Oh well, she had time. She'd go to the Tax Office right after. "We'll maybe get a Co-Cola or something. If that's all right with you."

"Oh, I couldn't let you do that. I don't want to impose."

"I'm offering. Cathy and I will get along just fine. You concentrate on getting the job."

Julia nodded. She stood up a little straighter.

Bruce's eyes looked glassy. Mrs. Entwhistle had seen him take a tiny white pill from his pocket and swallow it. She didn't say anything. None of her business. It had certainly mellowed Bruce out. No longer frantic with claustrophobia, he was in a talkative mood.

"You know what?" he asked rhetorically. "When I was this kid's age, Cathy's age, I wanted to be a teacher. I'd line up all my stuffed animals and play school. Didn't have no brothers or sisters, so stuffed animals were it. I'd put papers and pencils in front of 'em and I'd stand up in front and be the teacher."

"Why didn't you pursue it?" Judge Abernathy asked.

"Because my name is Bruce. Damn. Feathers. AKA Tickle-Feathers. AKA Goosey-Brucey. A boy named that, he can't look weak, you know? I was small for my age and I had to fight just about every recess from third grade on. Some kid would think I was a wimp and it was safe to make fun of my name, and I'd have to fight. That's how my school days went. You don't get to be no teacher like that, man."

"What about now?" Mrs. Entwhistle asked. "You're

150

still very young. Are you even twenty yet? You could go to college now and become a teacher."

"Yeah. No. I dropped out of high school in my junior year. Started working at the Harley shop. Got my own hog. Takes all my paycheck some weeks to keep it running."

"Still…could you study for your GED? And then maybe get into a community college and work toward your teaching certificate? Seems to me you'd be a great role model for kids like yourself who have it hard. You could relate."

"Takes money, lady. And time. And smarts. I ain't got any of that."

Mrs. Entwhistle nodded. "All right, then," she said. She didn't believe in trying to talk people into things. They either figured it out themselves, or they didn't. Judge Abernathy was frowning. He was used to issuing orders that had to be followed. But as the judge opened his mouth to speak, Bruce Feathers' chin dropped to his chest and suddenly he was asleep. The judge sighed.

"I see kids like him every day," he said quietly. "I hope I never see this one for anything more than a noise violation." But he didn't sound hopeful.

Allie and Lawrence were carrying on a whispered conversation, heads close together in their corner of the elevator. Occasionally, words shot forth like little bullets.

"… sick and tired…"

"You always…

"You never…"

"…waited all these years…"

151

"Wasted my time…"

Everyone looked away and pretended they couldn't hear. Mrs. Entwhistle searched her mind frantically for a topic of conversation. She asked Cathy what her favorite movie was. This resulted in the little girl becoming Elsa for a rendition of, "Let it gooooo, let it goooo," sung in piercing childish soprano. It did afford the squabbling couple a little privacy, but almost drowned out the shouts. Judge Abernathy held up one finger to signal quiet, and then they all heard it: "Hello, the elevator! Anybody in there?"

"Yes! We're here! Help, help!" they chorused.

"Okay, hang on, we're gonna get you out."

But instead, the elevator cab jerked and then dropped precipitously. They all yelled except Bruce, who only groaned. Suddenly, the indicator lit up with the news that they were now on the main floor. The doors didn't open, however, until their rescuers pried them apart with crowbars. The little group watched breathlessly as the panels parted, only to be confronted by a solid concrete wall. Four feet above them was the threshold into the main floor hallway.

A face appeared, peering down at them. "I'll get a ladder, have you out of there in no time," the face's owner said. "Don't go anywhere!"

"A little elevator humor," Mrs. Entwhistle said.

"Not very funny," Julia added.

The ladder was lowered and steadied at each end. Mrs. Entwhistle, the oldest, was helped to climb up and out first, followed by Cathy and her mother, then Allie and Lawrence. Bruce had to be manhandled up by Judge Abernathy. Mrs. Entwhistle wouldn't have given a wooden nickel for Bruce's chances of beating his ticket.

They blinked in the bright sunlight flooding the lobby where they stood. Allie and Lawrence were the first to leave, heading in opposite directions without a word to each other or anyone else.

"One less item on your docket," Mrs. Entwhistle murmured to the judge.

Bruce was waking up, looking confused and very young. Judge Abernathy took him by the arm. "Come along, young man," he said. "You've got a court appearance. But we'll take the stairs this time."

Mrs. Entwhistle took Cathy's small hand in hers.

"You go on to your interview," she said to Julia. "Cathy and I will wait for you in the snack bar. Good luck."

Neither Mrs. Entwhistle nor Julia Roberts found it strange that Cathy was being left in the care of a virtual stranger. Their shared elevator experience had swept away normal boundaries.

"I hope I never have to ride in a lelevator again," Cathy said. "They're scary."

"Oh, they're not so scary," Mrs. Entwhistle said. "Maybe the one we had today was just grouchy. Say, do you know why the elevator was in a bad mood?"

"No, why?"

"People were always pushing its buttons."

Cathy looked up at Mrs. Entwhistle in puzzlement. "But that's how you make it go," she said.

"Never mind," Mrs. Entwhistle said, swinging the little girl's hand. "Let's see about that Coke."

Mrs. Entwhistle Goes With the Wind

Mrs. Entwhistle jumped when the phone rang. Calls at night usually didn't mean good news, in her experience, and she picked up the phone apprehensively.

"Hello?"

"Mama, it's Tommy. Did I wake you?"

"No, son, I'm just watching television. That show I like is on, that one where the people sing and the judges can't see them, and then if they like them, they turn their chairs around…"

"Yes, Mama, I know which one you mean. Can you pause it?"

"It's just commercials right now. Why are you calling?"

"Well, we're in a bit of a crisis here at the theater."

Mrs. Entwhistle couldn't get used to Tommy being an actor. What an idea. She knew he needed to get out of the house since Judy left him, and she guessed amateur theatricals were one way to do it. Tommy had always been given to drama, when she thought about it. Maybe this was a good outlet for him. But still…

"You know we're staging an adaptation of *Gone With the Wind*. It's a spoof, a take-off; remember me telling you about it? Well, the gal who was playing Mammy fell downstairs at home and broke her nose. There's no way she can go onstage until the swelling goes down. So now we're just three days away from the first performance, and no Mammy," Tommy said.

"Huh. Too bad. What are you going to do?" Mrs. Entwhistle asked.

"Well, we've been talking about it and I was wondering if you'd fill in," Tommy said.

"Fill in? Tommy, what are you thinking? I'm not an actor."

"But this is a very easy part. Mammy is just kind of a walk-on, walk-off character. You'd be in full costume - a big long dress and apron and a do-rag around your head."

"A what?"

"You know, a kind of turban. And you'd only have a couple of lines. One time, you'd say, 'Good gracious, Miss Scarlet, you gon' get in trouble with that Rhett-fella.' Another time, 'Miss Scarlett, you got to eat.' Mammy is, like, an old family retainer, a servant, you know. You'd be great. You have a loud, I mean carrying, voice anyway, so you're already ahead of most of the cast."

"Is Mammy supposed to be old?" Mrs. Entwhistle asked.

"About your age, Mama, not old-old. I mean, she's a mature lady."

"Tommy, your favor-asking skills could use some work."

"I'm sorry, Mama. We're desperate, I mean, we'd be so excited to have you in the cast."

"Let me sleep on it."

Mrs. Entwhistle wanted to say no right that minute, but she thought about it. She'd been feeling distanced from her son ever since he and Diane had confiscated her car in that high-handed, uppity manner. Yes, she'd gotten it back, but a tinge of coolness had characterized her relationship with her children since. Maybe doing him this one little favor would lead to reestablishing warmth. The next morning, she called Tommy back and said she'd do it.

And so it was that Mrs. Entwhistle found herself backstage the next evening. The other cast members, while kind and welcoming to Tom's mother, were full of inside jokes and stage jargon. She felt unsure and out of place. But she listened dutifully to the director explain her part. It really was just as Tommy'd described: make two entrances, say two sentences, exit. Mrs. Entwhistle felt her customary self-confidence reassert itself. She could do this. Why did people make such a big deal about acting?

When her cue came, she strode onto the stage, belted out her line and departed to a smattering of applause from the rest of the cast. There was nothing to it. She sat backstage, following along in the script as she waited for her second and final appearance. She noticed a middle-aged woman who called out lines when needed. Goodness, you'd think people would know their parts by now.

The next night was dress rehearsal. Mrs. Entwhistle's costume was made for a much larger woman, but she'd anticipated as much and came supplied with safety pins. Once the fabric was taken in with pins, she'd baste in the alterations at home. The cue-lady, Teresa, helped her.

"You're Tom's mother?" she asked, pinning away.

"That's right. Tommy is my eldest, and he has a younger sister. All grown up now, but still my children," Mrs. Entwhistle said. "Do you have kids?"

"I have a teenage girl, Amanda. She's been, well, let's say a bit disturbed since her father and I split up. Acting out, you know."

"Oh, I know. They act out even if there's not a divorce. I could tell you some things about mine. But it passes; they grow up and get some sense eventually. The trick is to ride it out without losing your mind."

There was a pause, during which Teresa cleared her throat a couple of times. Then she said, "I don't know if Tom's told you, but we've been seeing each other."

"Seeing, as in dating?"

"Yes. I hope you don't mind."

"Why would I mind? None of my business. Actually, I'd be glad for Tommy to have some enjoyment in his life. He's been through a tough time."

"Yes, but even so, Tom's a lot of fun."

Mrs. Entwhistle digested this in silence. Fun and Tommy were not two words often used in the same sentence. He was a good man, Tommy was, but inclined to silence and morose moods like his father before him.

But if this woman – Teresa, was it? – thought he was fun, so much the better.

The backstage door opened with a whoosh of wind that sent script pages fluttering. Framed dramatically in the opening stood a girl. She was dressed in black, head to toe. Light glinted off the metal piercings that studded her face and ears. Her hair, slicked straight up from her forehead in a high crest, was bright green. Mrs. Entwhistle heard a sigh.

"My daughter," said Teresa. She motioned for the girl to come over. "Mrs. Entwhistle, I'd like you to meet Amanda. 'Manda, this is Tom's mother."

Amanda regarded Mrs. Entwhistle narrowly. "Yeah, Tom said his mommy was going to play Mammy."

Not pleased to meet you or kiss my foot, Mrs. Entwhistle thought. "How do you do?" is what she said.

"Do you have your costume?" Teresa asked her daughter.

"I'm standing in it," Amanda said.

"Oh, no…you're not going onstage like that! Are you?"

"Look, I'm an alternative Scarlett, remember? This is how I'm supposed to look."

"But it's how you look every day…."

"Exactly."

Amanda wandered over to the director, who held her at arm's length and looked her up and down, seemingly delighted with her appearance. Amanda shot a triumphant look at her mother. Mrs. Entwhistle sent up a silent prayer of thanksgiving that her child-rearing days were behind her.

Dress rehearsal went smoothly. Mrs. Entwhistle entered the stage on cue, said her lines in a strong, clear voice and exited. Easy-peasy. She watched the entire play from the wings and admitted to herself that she was puzzled. The old *Gone with the Wind* that she'd loved first as a book and later on the movie screen, was – well, gone with the wind. This adaptation, or spoof, or whatever it was, depicted Scarlett as a modern Goth teenage girl. Amanda really could and did play the part in her every-day street clothes. Tommy was Rhett and played him as an unsavory predator lusting after jail-bait. The sweeping love story was now reduced to leering one-liners. Mrs. Entwhistle found the whole thing distressing. But Tommy seemed to be having a good time, and she reminded herself that she was doing this for him.

The night of the performance approached without any particular nervous tremors on Mrs. Entwhistle's part. She arrived at the theater in plenty of time, changed into her costume and settled down in the wings to wait for her cue. The audience rustled and coughed on the other side of the curtain. Curious, Mrs. Entwhistle peeked. She drew back in surprise: there were actually people out there. And quite a lot of them. The theater seemed to be full. Who would have thought folks would actually turn out for such as this? She felt the first little fluttering in her stomach.

All too soon, it was time for her entrance. Her heart thudding, she walked cautiously onto the stage. When she opened her mouth to speak her line, nothing came out. Her mouth seemed to be lined with flannel. She gulped and tried again. A tiny voice, surely not her own, said, "Good gracious, Miss Scarlett...."and stopped. What came next? She glanced wildly at Teresa, waiting in the wings with script in hand. "…you gon' get in trouble with that Rhett-fella…" Teresa said softly. Mrs. Entwhistle nodded and repeated the words in a low monotone. The audience stirred, straining to hear. She exited, wet with sweat, hands shaking. Tommy met her backstage.

"Mama, are you okay? What happened?"

"I don't know, son. I could hear the audience out there behind the lights and I just came all over hot and cold. I've never had such a feeling before," Mrs. Entwhistle said, fanning herself vigorously with her script.

"That's just stage fright, Mama," Tommy said, patting her back reassuringly. "You'll be fine now that you've gotten your feet wet."

But she wasn't. The thought of going back out on that stage seemed impossible. And after all, she was an old woman. She shouldn't be subjected to such stress. It could bring on a stroke or something.

Mrs. Entwhistle sought out the director. "I seem to have lost my voice," she whispered to him.

He looked at her distractedly. "Just do what you did in rehearsal," he said, turning to another cast member. She was stuck. Short of making a run for it, she'd have to go out on that stage again.

Cora Entwhistle, she said sternly to herself, *you just get a hold of yourself right now. Floyd would have a fit if he saw you acting like such a big baby. All you have to do is walk out there and say one line. You said you'd do it for Tommy, and now you just buck up and do it.*

When the prop mistress stuck a plate of fake food in her hands, she walked determinedly onto the stage, heels hitting hard. "Miz Scarlett, you got to eat," she roared, slapping the plate down on the table. Amanda was so startled by the commanding tone that she almost ate a piece of plastic meatloaf. Mrs. Entwhistle turned and strode off the stage to applause and laughter from the audience.

"It wasn't supposed to be a funny scene," the director said. "But we'll take laughs wherever we can get 'em."

Mrs. Entwhistle sank into the nearest chair, feeling a great wash of relief. She thanked all the stars in the sky that the woman who normally played Mammy would be back for the remaining performances. She'd kept her promise to Tommy; now she just wanted to go home. Gradually, she became aware of an urgently whispered conversation between Tommy and Teresa.

"She doesn't like me," Tommy was saying. "I've been as nice to her as I know how to be, but she just doesn't like me."

"No, now, it's not that, Tom. Really. She's just...shy," Teresa said.

"Shy! Shy like a wolverine. I think she sees me as being like the role I'm playing – an old lecher. I guess I can't blame her. She's basically playing herself, and maybe she thinks I am, too."

Just then Amanda made her final exit to applause and cheers from the audience. The entire cast lined up to take a bow, Mrs. Entwhistle included. The level of enthusiasm was inexplicable, but she could only conclude that these people had never been exposed to the real *Gone With the Wind*. Now that it was all over, she'd survived, and she'd never have to do it again, she was enjoying herself. She even agreed to go along to the bar where everyone hung out after performances.

There she found herself sitting beside Amanda, who was surely too young to be in a bar, but nobody seemed concerned. She was staring at her cell phone and drinking a Diet Coke. Mrs. Entwhistle got one, too. They sipped in silence for a few minutes. Then Mrs. Entwhistle said, "He's not, you know."

"Who's not what?" Amanda asked, reasonably enough.

"Tommy. Tom. He's not an old lecher like Rhett in the play."

"I never said he was," Amanda said.

"But maybe you kind of thought it?" Mrs. Entwhistle said.

Amanda looked away. "I miss my Dad," she said, and it was not a non sequitur to Mrs. Entwhistle.

"I expect you do," she said. "It must be tough, parents splitting up and you don't want to take sides."

"I just think it would be better for Mom not to date," Amanda said.

"Better for her? Or easier for you?"

"Why do things have to change?" Amanda demanded angrily.

"I wish I knew," Mrs. Entwhistle said. "But that's life, isn't it? Everything changes, and all we can do is hang on and do the best we can. You'll be all right, you know. In a couple of years, you'll be off to college and then your adult life will begin. The important thing right now is to behave in a way that you can feel good about later on, when you look back. You don't have to feel it, just do it. You're an actress, right?"

"But isn't that dishonest? Shouldn't we be up front with our feelings?"

"Heavens, no!" Mrs. Entwhistle said with a laugh. "That would lead to chaos. No, in a bad situation, what we can do is figure out the kind of behavior we'd admire if we were watching someone else, and do that. Eventually, you may feel it, but even if you don't, you'll never regret taking the high road."

"Mmm," said Amanda. Mrs. Entwhistle knew that was all she was going to get in the way of agreement. But maybe a seed had been planted. In any case, she'd spoken the truth as she knew it, and done what she could for Tommy. However his relationship with Teresa and Amanda turned out, it was beyond her control.

Suddenly exhausted, she knew it was time to go home. She waved to Tommy across the room, fished in her purse for her car keys and headed for the door. Just for a second, she struggled with the temptation to raise her fist and shout, "As God is my witness, I'll never act in a play again!"

High road, she told herself. *High road.*

Maxine and the Nigerian Prince

Mrs. Entwhistle wasn't exactly tech-savvy. In fact, if Tommy hadn't helped her set up her e-mail account, she wouldn't have had one. Facebook? That was a sorrowful mystery to her. Like Dorothy in Oz, she felt that things seemed to come and go so quickly there. She didn't post much herself, but she enjoyed seeing what her grandchildren were up to. Their postings were becoming fewer and fewer, though.

"It's because all the old folks are on Facebook now," Maxine told her. "Kids don't want to be where we are, so now they're on Tweeter or Snoop-Chat, or I don't know what-all."

But the ladies did the best they could, and particularly enjoyed the Internet's ever-present answers to any questions that might cross their minds. Maxine tended to believe everything she read, on the grounds that if it wasn't true, why would somebody write it? Mrs. Entwhistle was apt to be skeptical.

They were sitting on Mrs. Entwhistle's porch swing on a red and gold autumn morning, swinging gently as they sipped their third cups of tea. Maxine was reading her tablet. Mrs. Entwhistle hadn't invested in one. Going to her desk where the keyboard and BAM lived wasn't that inconvenient. BAM was what Tommy called it. She'd asked him once what it stood for, and he'd said Big-Ass Monitor. After that, she didn't inquire too much into acronyms.

"Says here," Maxine reported with furrowed brow, "that we should be brushing our teeth sideways, like we did when we were kids."

"Why, I remember when our tenth-grade health teacher, Mrs. Lenneke, taught us the proper way to brush was down. It was awkward, but I've gotten used to it," Mrs. Entwhistle said. "Now we're supposed to go back to the old way?"

"And remember when they added the words, 'under God,' to the Pledge of Allegiance?" Maxine said. "We were in the tenth grade then, too. That was an eventful year."

They shook their heads over the fickle ways of the world. Mrs. Entwhistle heard the ping that announced a new e-mail on Maxine's tablet, and saw Maxine's back stiffen to attention as she read it.

"Cora! Look at this!"

Maxine sounded upset. Mrs. Entwhistle looked.

"You are reached because friend say you are trusted. Friend is Giancarlo Cisserino. I am Ali Zaki Askya, prince of Nigerian royal family, who seeks to come to your great country to escape death here. Government wish to

165

kills me because I am of royal family and they fear people rally to me to overthrow corrupt regime. I must seek asylums. I have 150 million naira, is $100 million U.S. dollars, but banks here I cannot trust. I ask the great favor to use your bank account to accept my money. This money saves me and my family to escape. In return, I give you $1 million U.S. dollars when I come to your country. You check with Reginald Osbourne of Bank of England, he vouch for me, but cannot help because banking regulations. Reach him at rosbourne@bankmail.com. He expects hearing from you. We must hurry! Lifes are in danger. Please to send routing number of your bank account so I can make deposit. You hold for me please, I will come to you and give one million. You are saving my life and family life, also babies."

Maxine's eyes were huge behind her trifocals. "It sounds like the poor man is in terrible danger," she said.

Mrs. Entwhistle looked at her to see if she was kidding. What she saw was sincere concern. "Max," she said gently, "It's a well-known scam, honey. This guy isn't a real prince. If he gets into your bank account, he'll clean you out. Then he'll disappear."

"Oh, I don't think so, in this case," Maxine said, "because he said Giancarlo is his friend."

"I don't know how this guy got Giancarlo's name, which, by the way, he misspelled, but I doubt if they know each other. And even if they do, think for a minute about Giancarlo. Remember, he's into scams himself."

"But we went to school with Giancarlo," Maxine said.

"Exactly. So what better way to earn your trust than to claim friendship with an old schoolmate?"

"I don't care about the $1 million," Maxine said slowly, "but I'd never forgive myself if I let a man die because I wouldn't help. And he said there are babies!"

"Max, for heaven's sake, that's not what's at stake here."

"Look, this reference is for a man at the Bank of England. That certainly sounds legitimate."

"Of course it does," Mrs. Entwhistle said. "It's meant to sound legitimate to sucker you in. Don't be a chump." Too late, she heard the exasperation in her own voice.

"I don't think I'm a chump because I care about saving lives," Maxine said. She rose, her mouth set in a straight line, and put her tablet in her purse.

"I'm going to go on now. See you later, I guess."

"No, now, Max, don't be mad. Just check it out before you do anything. Go talk to Mr. Dansinger at the bank."

Maxine's heels hit harder than usual as she made her way across the porch toward her car in the driveway. Roger looked up reproachfully when his pal passed him by without so much as an ear-scratch.

Mrs. Entwhistle called after her, "Maxine, wait up. I'll go with you, we'll go to the bank..." But Maxine was gone.

~*~

Mrs. Entwhistle went to the bank herself. She didn't

see Maxine's car in the parking lot and felt a stab of fear that her friend had already acted. Mr. Dansinger looked up from his computer screen with squinty eyes when Mrs. Entwhistle approached his desk. The bank was so small that the president's office was right off the lobby. Mr. Dansinger prided himself on having an open door policy. He liked to say that anybody could walk into the bank and talk to him at any time. Mrs. Entwhistle had never been more thankful that she lived in a small town where this was possible.

"Mr. Dansinger," she began. But his upraised hand stopped her.

"Now, Mrs. Entwhistle, you call me Erroll," he said. "We've had this conversation before. You've known me since I was a little boy, there's no need to 'mister' me."

"Well, yes, I grew up with your father, but you're president of the bank now, and I respect that," Mrs. Entwhistle said firmly. "Let me tell you why I've come. It's about Maxine Jones."

Mr. Dansinger listened without interrupting. "So you think Mrs. Jones has been taken in by this scheme?" he asked.

"I'm afraid so. It's her soft heart, you know. Maxine's not greedy for money, and she's no dummy, but her heart rules her head every time. She thinks if she doesn't help this guy, he'll be killed. She thinks it's up to her to save him. I know her; I know how her mind works."

"Hmmm. I see." Erroll Dansinger turned to his keyboard, typed rapidly, and then surveyed the screen. "No activity as of yet," he said. "I'm taking the liberty of freezing the account."

Mrs. Entwhistle blew out a breath of relief. Her shoulders descended from up under her ears, where they'd resided since the Nigerian prince's e-mail first hit Maxine's tablet.

"Now," he said, "her money is safe for the moment." He paused and gazed thoughtfully at the ceiling. "Did you know Mrs. Jones was my Sunday School teacher when I was in middle school? I was a mess back then, but she was unfailingly kind - a bright spot in my life when I needed one. I'd never want to make her feel stupid or incompetent."

Mrs. Entwhistle had forgotten Max taught Sunday School all those years ago. You never knew what consequences were going to show up in the future, she mused. Scratch Mr. Dansinger, stodgy middle-aged banker, and find an unhappy boy with a long memory.

Mr. Dansinger beckoned to a young man standing behind the teller window. "Chris, come here a minute, would you please? I need your help." He turned back to Mrs. Entwhistle. "I'm not too bad on the computer, but Chris, here, he can do anything."

Chris looked about sixteen to Mrs. Entwhistle, who deplored the trend she'd been noticing for some years, of children running the world. But here was this pimply youth all done up in a coat and tie, obviously a trusted bank employee. She sighed.

Mr. Dansinger explained the situation. "So we need to get a message to Mrs. Jones that will look like it came from this so-called Nigerian prince. Can you do that?"

"Sure, no problem," young Chris said easily. "What do you want it to say?"

~*~

Mrs. Entwhistle drove directly to Maxine's house. Over the many years of their friendship, they'd had so few spats she couldn't even remember the last one. But today she knew she'd hurt her old friend when she'd spoken to her as if she were, in Mr. Dansinger's words, stupid and incompetent. Mrs. Entwhistle felt a little fluttering of nerves as she approached Maxine's door, and that made her pause and knock instead of walking in, calling "Yoo-hoo," as she normally did.

Maxine came to the door carrying her tablet. "Oh, Cora, I'm so glad you're here. You'll never believe what's happened. Come in, come in, honey."

As if her feelings had never been hurt, as if she'd never stalked off the porch and driven off without a word. Mrs. Entwhistle's stomach unknotted. That was Maxine; not a grudging bone in her body.

"Look here at this new e-mail I got from Prince Askya," Max said.

She held out her tablet and Mrs. Entwhistle read:

"I am getting back to you to say all is well with me now. My father, the king, has taken over the government in my land, and we are safe. There is no longer need for me to get my money out of Nigeria. Long live my father, long live the king!"

"Well, I swanee," Mrs. Entwhistle said. "Isn't that grand! You don't have to worry about him one more minute."

"Yes, it's just amazing timing," Maxine said. "I was actually about to send him my bank information when I got

170

this. You can tell by the way he wrote that he's relieved; even his English improved."

Mrs. Entwhistle bit the inside of her cheek to stop a smile.

"I'll confess," Maxine continued, "that I was a little scared about helping him after you seemed so sure it was a scam. I even tried to check with that man at the Bank of England, but my message came back marked undeliverable. Then I was afraid to wait any longer. I couldn't bear the thought that the prince or his family – there are babies! - might be killed because I dilly-dallied. I said to myself, Maxine, do what you know is right. Just then the second e-mail came, and now it's all worked out fine." She beamed at Mrs. Entwhistle. "We'll have to look up the Nigerian royal family on the Internet. Maybe we'll see a picture of the prince."

"You know, I think we ought to just let it go," Mrs. Entwhistle said. "No sense in worrying about what happens on the other side of the world. Things change so fast, it's hard enough to keep up with politics here at home, don't you think?"

"Maybe you're right," Maxine said. "You often are."

Mrs. Entwhistle heard Max whisper, "Although you weren't this time."

Mrs. Entwhistle Wins the Sweepstakes

Mrs. Entwhistle blinked into the sunlight at the strangers on her doorstep. One of them was holding an enormous bouquet of balloons; another clutched a fistful of red roses. A woman, dressed fit to kill, jumped up and down on her stiletto heels in a way that looked unsafe. She was holding a large cardboard rectangle. There were several vehicles at the curb, including a van with some kind of tower on the top. What in the world?

Roger arrived at the door and sized up the assemblage as well as he could with his milky old eyes. "Wuf," he said, and then turned back to his new bed. He purely loved the fleece bed Mrs. Entwhistle brought home when his arthritis got too bad for leaps up onto the couch. For years he'd loved his naps on the couch, and now he loved his naps in the new bed. Dogs were so accepting. No doubt the couch was better off without his constant presence - it certainly smelled better - but still, she felt bad for him. It's hard to watch a good dog grow old. Mrs. Entwhistle brought her attention back to the puzzling spectacle unfolding before her.

A furry knob on a long stick was thrust toward Mrs. Entwhistle's face. The woman was dancing, waggling the piece of cardboard. All of them were showing a lot of very white teeth. Floyd used to say grins like that reminded him of a mule eating briars.

"Cora Enthissle?" said the man who seemed to be the leader.

"It's Entwhistle," she replied.

"Cora Entwhistle, this is your lucky day! You've just won the Publishers' Clearinghouse Sweepstakes!"

"Oh, no, I don't think so," Mrs. Entwhistle said. "I didn't buy any magazines, and I didn't enter."

"No purchase is necessary, ma'am!" the woman said. "Look here, your name is on this check!"

These people seemed to speak only in exclamations. Mrs. Entwhistle smiled politely. "I'm sure you're mistaken," she said. "Thank you, anyway." She started to close the door.

"NO!"

The heartfelt, horror-stricken chorus made her pause.

"You really have won, Mrs. Entwhistle! You are the winner of One! Million! Dollars!"

By now, the neighbors had come out on their front porches, craning their necks to see what the disturbance was about. Mrs. Entwhistle saw Ronnie Sue and motioned for her to come over.

"Ronnie Sue, honey, could you come help me a little bit?" she said. "These folks have made a mistake and

I can't seem to get through to them."

But then Ronnie Sue was jumping up and down, too, grabbing Mrs. Entwhistle in such a bear hug they nearly fell off the step. "You DID win, Mrs. Entwhistle! You're rich, you're rich!" she screamed.

"But I never entered…"

"I entered your name," Ronnie Sue confessed. "Biff and I did it. Just for fun. And now you've won!"

"Well, my stars," Mrs. Entwhistle said, sinking down on the nearest porch chair.

~*~

What she did as soon as everyone left was call Maxine. Then afterwards, she felt guilty that she hadn't called her children first. But it was just so natural to share everything with Maxine. She was there within minutes, swinging into the driveway with more than usual panache. After the first flurry of exclamations were over and Mrs. Entwhistle had explained it all as best she could, the two ladies had a restorative cup of tea at the kitchen table.

"What will you do with all that money, Cora?" Max asked, her eyes sparkling.

"Why, I don't know," Mrs. Entwhistle said. "What do you think I should do? Do you need some of it? Because you're welcome to as much as you want."

"Oh, no, Cora, no, I don't need it, but thank you." Maxine said, smiling.

Despite sharing almost everything else, the friends didn't discuss their sex lives or their personal finances. Mrs. Entwhistle knew when Maxine's husband passed, there'd been a big insurance policy; Maxine had said that much when she purchased her Lincoln. And Floyd had provided well for her. She had a share of his pension from forty years at the Bell Bomber plant, and, now that he was gone, half his Social Security. That was plenty for her day-to-day expenses. True, she had only ten thousand dollars in savings, and she'd been ready to sacrifice that to get Roger back when he was kidnapped. Or would it be dognapped? Still, ten thousand wasn't very much of a cushion these days. If she needed a new roof, or the furnace gave out, or the basement sprang a leak, why, poof! - that money would be gone. So it would be nice to have more in the bank, but one million? No, she didn't need that much.

"I'd better talk to Diane and Tommy," she said.

~*~

Diane shed tears when she heard her mother's news. "Oh, Mama," she said, "what a relief to know the kids' college costs are taken care of! We've just been saving as hard as we can, but we could never have come up with it all."

Mrs. Entwhistle blinked at the immediate assumption that her money was Diane's money, but she let it pass. Of course, she'd be glad to help with her grandchildren's educations.

"Yeah, my kids'll be needing it, too," Tommy said. "I'm not good enough to live with them, but I'm still on the hook for college." He sounded bitter, but that was the way he always sounded since Judy took the two little girls and left him. It was a hard row to hoe, Mrs. Entwhistle agreed, paying for a decision his ex-wife had made alone.

"First thing I'll do is establish college funds for each of the grandchildren," she said. "I'm going down to the bank tomorrow morning and talk to Mr. Dansinger about how to set things up."

"My car's got almost 200,000 miles on it," Tommy said hopefully.

"We had to take out a second mortgage last year when Jack lost his job," Diane added. They both looked at their mother the way they used to in the toy aisle of Wal-Mart.

~*~

Ronnie Sue was sitting on Mrs. Entwhistle's porch steps when she got back from the bank the next morning. She was crying. Not unusual. Ronnie Sue was a crier, no doubt about that, but Mrs. Entwhistle sensed these weren't superficial tears.

"You better tell me what's wrong," she said, resting her hand on Ronnie Sue's smooth head.

"It's Mama, and it's – oh, just everything," Ronnie Sue said, sniffing in a way that made Mrs. Entwhistle produce her own ironed cloth hankie "She's just not getting better, and the treatments make her feel so bad. I don't know what to do."

"Why, Ronnie Sue, I think you're doing just fine by your mama," Mrs. Entwhistle said. "You handle all the cooking and cleaning, and take her to the doctor and the chemo place. I'd say you are a mighty big comfort to her."

"Thank you, ma'am, but…"

Mrs. Entwhistle waited.

"See, Biff and I – we want to get married. We don't have to," Ronnie Sue added hastily, "but we're out of high school now and we've got jobs, and well, we just don't want to wait any longer. But Mama needs me at home, and I don't know how long she'll need me, and I don't want her life to end just so mine can begin! And yet, it's so hard to waaaaait." The sobs became wails.

Mrs. Entwhistle patted Ronnie Sue's back automatically. She was thinking. She knew Ronnie Sue's part-time job was at the Curl-E-Cue Corner, where she shampooed customers and swept up around the chairs. Biff worked at the car wash. Together, they didn't make enough money to support themselves, never mind any future additions. But both were good workers. She remembered Biff's efforts right here at her house, when he was earning money to pay off his drug dealer. He'd not known how to do the simplest things then, but showed an eagerness to learn that warmed Mrs. Entwhistle's heart. As for Ronnie Sue, she'd come a long way since the night she'd tried to steal Mrs. Entwhistle's Social Security money. The two youngsters had grown up very satisfactorily in the last couple of years, but now they were trying to start their adult lives too soon, and with a couple of strikes against them right from the get-go.

"Didn't you used to say you wanted to be a hair stylist?" Mrs. Entwhistle asked.

"Yes, but you have to complete a training course, and then you have to get a license and all." Ronnie Sue was still sniffling, but she seemed to have regained at least some of her composure.

"What about Biff? Does he like his job at the car wash?

"No, he hates it. He always wanted to be – I know it sounds icky – a plumber. He likes figuring out how pipes and things fit together, says it's like a Rubik's Cube. He's good at stuff like that, too. He talks about having his own plumbing company and me working in the office."

Mrs. Entwhistle spoke slowly. "Now listen here, Ronnie Sue. What if you both had a trade, a skill that would make you a good living? Wouldn't that be better than just make-shift jobs? Wouldn't you be willing to postpone marriage for that?"

Ronnie Sue considered. She said, "Sure, I'd be willing to wait, and if I said so, Biff would be, too. But the thing is, it would take years before we could even start training. We'd have to save up first."

"I want you and Biff to find out what it takes to become a plumber, and to get a hairdressing license. Then I want you to come and tell me. It will be my pleasure to pay for your training."

"Oh, Mrs. Entwhistle, I was never hinting!" Ronnie Sue's eyes were twin saucers of horror.

"I know you weren't, honey. But I wouldn't even have all this money if not for you and Biff. I'd love to pay you back a little bit."

~*~

The phone rang at nine p.m., just as Mrs. Entwhistle was starting to watch Hawaii Five-O. She and Maxine were faithful viewers. They loved the scenery. Neither lady had ever visited any place remotely tropical, and they were fans of the chameleon ocean and graceful palm trees. Now she glanced at the clock before reaching for the television remote and pausing the program. Who'd call so late?

"Cora? Cora Entwhistle?"

"Who's calling?"

"Why, Cora, don't you recognize my voice? It's Giancarlo. Giancarlo Cicerino."

"Oh. Are you calling from California? It's nine p.m. here. What do you want?"

"Come on, Cora, you're not that old! Nine p.m., so what? It's cocktail time here, and I was just lifting a glass and thinking of you. Can't an old friend call an old friend? Does there have to be a reason?"

"But there is a reason, isn't there?"

"Just wanted to congratulate you on winning the Publishers' Clearinghouse."

"How did you hear about that?"

"Oh, the old high-school grapevine, you know. Great thing for you, great thing. Change your life, am I right? No telling what you'll get up to now, with all that money. I bet old Fuddy-Duddy Floyd is turning over in his grave."

Mrs. Entwhistle sent an icy silence through the telephone. The nerve of the man, calling Floyd by that hurtful old nickname. She had to bite her tongue to keep from retaliating with Floyd's name for him, Sissy-Pants Cicerino. But no, she wouldn't stoop to his level.

"So, I was wondering, do you have a good financial advisor? Because with that much money, you've got to be smart, not let it slip through your fingers. Need someone you know you can trust, am I right?"

"Mr. Dansinger at the bank is handling everything for me," Mrs. Entwhistle said in her frostiest voice.

"Oh, yeah, moss-back Dansinger. Knew his dad, Junior's just like him - conservative as they come. Probably got the first dollar he ever made. I gave him a great opportunity when I was out there for the reunion. Would have made that little bank of his rich, and him, too. Know what he said? He said, 'The bank does not speculate.' Pompous bastard. But you, now. You want your money to make money, am I right? I just heard of a sure thing, double your investment in six months, hardly any risk. Let me handle it for you, get you in on the ground floor…"

Mrs. Entwhistle gently placed the receiver back in the cradle of her old-fashioned desk phone. The last words she heard were, "am I right?" She reached for the remote.

~*~

She'd meant to visit the homeless shelter regularly, but it'd been months since she'd helped serve Christmas dinner. Patricia, Rachel and Mary. She remembered them vividly. The women and their obvious needs had made such an impression on her that she'd donated her spare coats, along with new gloves, boots and scarves for which she'd braved the after-Christmas crowds at Wal-Mart. But none of the three women had been there when she'd returned with her offerings. She'd left them at the front desk with a sinking feeling that they'd go in the big bin from which anybody could help themselves. Then, somehow, she'd never made it back. Now she parked in the gravel area in front of the shelter and went inside.

"Rachel? Patricia? Do you know their last names?"

the volunteer at the front desk asked.

"No, we never exchanged last names. I met them when I volunteered at Christmas dinner last year, but they were staying across town at the women's shelter. Well, Rachel had a tent somewhere, I believe. Mary was wearing an orthopedic boot."

"Oh, Mary Watson Yes, she's here. She may know where the others are. Mary's just gone into the common room. Straight ahead and on your left."

Mrs. Entwhistle entered the large, shabby room and looked around. She hoped she'd recognize Mary, but all the occupants looked worn, bedraggled and somehow alike. With relief, she saw a woman with one leg propped up on a stool. Mrs. Entwhistle made her way over to her.

"Mary, do you remember me? Cora Entwhistle? We met last Christmas and had lunch together."

"Why, 'course I do! Cora, that gave us a ride in her nice car to the women's shelter. Sit down, sit down."

Mrs. Entwhistle did, trying not to stare at Mary's leg. It was twice the size of a normal limb and wore a soiled, mummy-like wrapping from ankle to knee. Mary caught her looking.

"Oh, just my old bum leg," she said. "I got an infection between my toes last winter and it seems like it spread up my leg."

"Does it hurt?" Mrs. Entwhistle asked.

"It used to hurt real sharp, but mostly it's just numb now."

"Did a doctor look at it?"

"Oh, land's sake, no, not regular. Couldn't afford one, and the free clinic ran out of donations and had to close. But I can get around some. It don't bother me that much," Mary said cheerfully.

"Where are Patricia and Rachel?" Mrs. Entwhistle said. "I was hoping to find all three of you today."

"Who? Oh, you mean them that ate with us? Oh, they're long gone. Rachel said she was goin' to California to see if she could find her boys. And Patricia – I guess she just moved on. Said she was tired of the cold."

"But you stayed."

"Well, I didn't have much choice. Can't walk so far these days."

"Mary, I think you ought to have that leg looked at. Will you let me take you to the emergency department at the hospital?"

"Dearie, it don't do no good. I been there once before. The nurse just cleaned my leg up good and rewrapped it, gave me some pills for infection. She said to come back if it don't get better, but I hate to. They know I can't pay."

"This time it'll be different. Come on."

~*~

The West Side Senior Center was buzzing when Mrs. Entwhistle entered. There were two tables of bridge, one of beaders, another of scrapbookers and a quiet group huddled around the small television set in the corner. She approached the bridge table where her old Meals on Wheels clients, J.C., Angelina, Exeter and Myrna were deep into a game.

"Hi, everyone," she said.

"Shhhh!" J.C. said, holding up one imperious finger. "Wait until my partner finishes this hand."

Angelina looked up apologetically before returning her concentration to the cards on the table. Exeter and Myrna waggled their fingers, but didn't dare speak under J.C's stern gaze.

Mrs. Entwhistle wandered over to the beading table, where Thelma and Ramona bent their heads over elaborate necklaces. Thelma was still wearing pink.

"Thelma, Ramona," Mrs. Entwhistle said.

They looked up at her, blinking like sleepers awakened. "Oh, Cora, hello," they chorused.

"How did you all get here?" Mrs. Entwhistle asked.

"The county has a van that picks us up and takes us home," Thelma said, "and, oh, it's ever-so-handy, it comes right to the door and if you need help, the driver hops out and puts a little step in front of the door, and then he'll take your arm and give you a boost, you know, and we pick up everyone else and just have the best visit all the way here, and then we have lunch and stay for the afternoon, until the bus driver – Andy is his name – comes to take us home."

Thelma's loquaciousness hadn't diminished. "I see. Well, do you need anything? Got plenty to eat at home?" Mrs. Entwhistle said.

Thelma and Ramona looked puzzled. "Why, I don't think we need anything, do we, Thelma?"

Mrs. Entwhistle hoped that meant Ramona no longer smuggled cookies home for later.

183

"No, we've got everything we need," Thelma said. She couldn't keep from glancing down at her beading.

Mrs. Entwhistle noticed that the cards were being gathered up and reshuffled at the bridge table. She hurried back.

"Good game?"

"Hello, Cora. Sorry I couldn't speak a moment ago. Yes, all our games are good," Angeline said, smiling so deeply her dimples showed. "J.C. and I took that hand." She sent a look that could only be described as amorous across the table to her partner. Mrs. Entwhistle held her breath, expecting J. C. to say something mean. But his eyes softened and he patted Angelina's hand.

"That's my smart little partner," he said. Mrs. Entwhistle's jaw dropped; she snapped her mouth shut hurriedly.

Myrna added up the scores while Exeter dealt the next hand. All four heads bent over their cards again. Mrs. Entwhistle stood watching for a moment.

"Do any of you need anything?" she asked. "Not just right here and now, but at home?"

Myrna glanced up distractedly from the cards in her hand. "Oh, no, dear, we're all just fine. Exeter and I come here every day, and now that Angelina and J.C. have moved in together, they're here a lot, too. We can have a game just about any time we want."

"Moved in...? Well, congratulations." Mrs. Entwhistle said, anchoring her jaw once again.

But nobody was paying any attention to her. Angelina's lips moved as she counted her points. Exeter cleared his throat and started the bidding. Mrs. Entwhistle slipped away.

Remembering the day she and Max dragged all of them out for their first visit to the Senior Center, she grinned to herself. Life was entertaining. She approached the front desk and handed the receptionist a sealed white envelope.

"Would you please make sure this gets to the manager?" she said.

~*~

Pete Peters wasn't answering his cell phone, and after a couple days of failing to reach him, Mrs. Entwhistle drove to his house. She rang the doorbell and stood waiting, tapping her foot, but no one answered. That was odd, because it was Saturday and Pete's car was in the driveway. He was newly married and as far as Mrs. Entwhistle knew, his wife, Sheila, stayed home with the children. Pete had gotten himself two little boys along with their mother, so his life had changed drastically since his days as a bachelor Deputy U.S. Marshal. Mrs. Entwhistle had danced at his wedding, glad to know that her friend's life was full of people who loved him.

Voices led Mrs. Entwhistle around the side of the house into the back yard. There she found Sheila pushing little Max and Ian on a tire swing hanging from the oak tree. She paused a moment to watch the boys swoop back and forth with shrieks of mock terror. Sheila saw her and abandoned her post, letting the swing gradually wind down.

"Good morning," she said, approaching Mrs. Entwhistle. "Did you ring the front bell and no one came?

Sorry, I should rig up a backyard bell or at least leave a note on the door, because who could hear anything with these two around?"

"That's okay," Mrs. Entwhistle said. "I came because I haven't been able to reach Pete on his cell. Is everything all right?"

Sheila looked guilty. She didn't meet Mrs. Entwhistle's eyes. Mrs. Entwhistle waited. Finally, Sheila said, "He didn't want you to know, that's why he's been dodging your calls."

"Know what?"

"Pete's working two jobs now. In addition to the Marshal Service, he's working overnight at the convenience store on Route 30. He grabs a nap whenever he can. That's what he's doing right now, and why I have the boys out back."

"And here I come, ringing the doorbell," Mrs. Entwhistle said. "I hope he didn't hear it. Now tell me: why is Pete working two jobs?"

"It's for Ian," Sheila said. They both looked over at the little boy, now playing in the sandbox. Mrs. Entwhistle hadn't noticed before, but Ian's face was unnaturally pale and his lips had a bluish tinge.

"Is he sick?" she asked.

"He has a heart defect. He was born with it, but it couldn't be fixed until he was three. Pete put us on his insurance when we got married, but there will still be a big co-pay, so he's working like crazy to save for it. He won't hear of me getting a job, said I need to stay home with the boys. I feel bad, Mrs. Entwhistle. Our marriage has brought him so much trouble."

"Pete told me you and the boys are the best things that have ever happened to him," Mrs. Entwhistle said. "The important thing now is to get Ian fixed up and well. But no sense in Pete killing himself to do it. I'd like you to go in and wake him now. I have a proposition for both of you."

"Wake him? But…"

"Just do it, Sheila. I promise it will be okay."

~*~

"So, do you have anything left?" Maxine asked.

They'd just watched Diane and Tommy drive away in their new cars. Mrs. Entwhistle explained that Tommy needed a car and, well, she couldn't get him one and not Diane. And Diane had needed her second mortgage paid off, so Tommy should get an equal amount of cash. Only fair. The four grandchildren had scholarship accounts which would be earning interest until college time rolled around. And they each had a new bike, because kids should share in their grandma's good fortune in a way they could enjoy right now.

Ronnie Sue and Biff would start their apprenticeship programs at the beginning of next month. Biff was paying installments on a tiny diamond engagement ring. That was a secret only Mrs. Entwhistle knew.

The West Side Senior Center's new big-screen television arrived, compliments of an anonymous donor who'd left a cashier's check with the receptionist. No mere T.V. program could be as engrossing as the buzz of speculation about the donor's identity.

Mary was in rehab, learning to walk on her prosthetic leg. She'd go from there to a rent-controlled apartment in a seniors' complex, which she could afford now that she qualified for Social Security disability income.

Little Ian's heart surgery was scheduled. It didn't have to wait until his father earned extra money to cover the co-pay. And there'd be more expenses, because a new baby was on the way. Pete said they'd name her Cora if it was a girl, Floyd if it was a boy.

All in all, Mrs. Entwhistle couldn't remember when she'd had so much fun.

Now she answered Maxine's question. "Oh, sure, I have plenty left," she said. "There's a nice cushion in the bank, and how much do I need at my age?"

"Did you spend any of it on yourself?" Maxine asked.

She raised an inquiring eyebrow as Mrs. Entwhistle handed her an envelope. Inside were two first-class airline tickets to Hawaii.

Mrs. Entwhistle said. "I thought we'd go and see for ourselves."

ABOUT THE AUTHOR

Doris Reidy began her writing career in third grade, when a poem about fairies dancing in the moonlight made the local newspaper. (Rumor suggests it was a slow news day). In later years, she wrote non-fiction articles for *Redbook, Writer's Digest* and *Atlanta Magazine*, among others, and a monthly book review column for the *Atlanta Journal and Constitution*. Then came a long silence during which life intervened, followed by a second act as a novelist. After writing two novels, **Five for the Money** (nominated for the 2016 Georgia Author of the Year/First Novel award), and **Every Last Stitch** (nominated for the 2017 Georgia Author of the Year Award, Literary Fiction), she found a friend and muse in *Mrs. Entwhistle*. Please follow Doris Reidy on Facebook, her website, www.dorisreidy.com, and leave your feedback at reidybooks@gmail.com.

The first chapter of Mrs. Entwhistle's continuing adventures follows.

☐☐☐ · ☐☐☐☐☐☐☐☐☐
☐☐☐☐☐ ☐☐☐☐☐

☐☐☐☐☐☐☐ ☐☐☐
☐☐☐☐☐'☐ ☐☐☐☐☐☐☐ ☐☐☐☐☐
☐☐☐ ☐☐☐☐

Mrs. Entwhistle's cheerful yellow kitchen went dark for a minute as she took in the news. She gave herself a good shake and the darkness receded. This was no time to panic.

The registered letter was written in intimidating legalese which she had to read three times, the last time out loud. It seemed to be saying that Floyd's pension would be no more. Simply put, the pension fund in which Floyd invested faithfully for forty years had gone broke. Maybe she'd got it wrong. She needed an interpreter. She'd go see Mr. Dansinger at the bank. He'd be able to explain it properly.

Mr. Dansinger looked up with a smile when Mrs. Entwhistle entered. He stood courteously, motioned her to a seat in front of his desk, asked if he could get her anything – a cup of coffee, a bottle of water? – before he sat himself and asked what brought her to the bank that morning.

"I'm trying to figure out if this letter means what I think it means," she said, handing it over.

He read the letter silently. When he looked up, his eyes were full of concern.

"I'm afraid you got it right," he said gently. "It seems Floyd's former employer didn't keep up with his share of contributions to the pension fund. Now the business is going into bankruptcy and the pension fund is broke. It's a shame. Retirees have a right to count on funds that were promised to them, and to which they contributed."

"Floyd would have a fit," Mrs. Entwhistle murmured. She could imagine his indignation – no, his wrath – if this had happened during his time on Earth. He'd planned carefully for their old age and they did without many little luxuries so their retirement years would be comfortable. Poor Floyd hadn't lived long enough to really enjoy it, but Mrs. Entwhistle was thankful for the checks that arrived faithfully month after month from Floyd's lifelong employer. Now those checks would no longer be coming.

"Will you be all right?" Mr. Dansinger asked.

Mrs. Entwhistle knew he was genuinely concerned. His father had been their banker, and when he retired, the son took over. Their families had a long history of mutual trust.

"Well, it will take some readjusting," she admitted. "That was half my monthly income."

"Of course, you have the investment accounts from the Publisher's Clearinghouse win," Mr. Dansinger said. "The funds are in your grandchildren's names, but I'm sure they and their parents would agree to withdraw money for your use."

Mrs. Entwhistle had won a million dollars from Publisher's Clearinghouse which wasn't as much money as it used to be, she'd learned. By the time she'd paid taxes and shared with friends and family, there wasn't much left. She'd had so much fun spreading cash around that she privately admitted to her best friend, Maxine, she might have gotten a little carried away.

"But how much do I need, at my age?" she'd said at the time. Now it appeared she needed more than she'd thought. But her grandchildren's accounts were off limits.

"I won't touch those accounts," she said. "I promised that money to my grandchildren to give them a good start in life, and I won't ask for it back. No, I'll have to come up with income from some other source. Let me go home and think on it."

~*~

Ordinarily, the first thing Mrs. Entwhistle did in times of trouble was call Maxine. They'd shared so many experiences over the years: school days, motherhood, widowhood, and now retirement. Mrs. Entwhistle frequently said there never was a better friend than Max. But her hand faltered as she reached for her phone. Two things she and Maxine never discussed were sex and money. They came from a generation reticent about such personal matters. The only time money had ever been mentioned between them was when Roger, Mrs. Entwhistle's aged Shih 'Tzu, was taken and held for ransom. Mrs. Entwhistle had been grateful, but she'd declined Maxine's offer of cash and handled it herself. She'd do the same thing now.

She sat down at her desk, pulled out her last bank statement and tapped numbers into the calculator. It didn't take a mathematical genius to see that Social Security income alone was not enough. Mrs. Entwhistle had never worked outside the home, but she got half of Floyd's benefit after his death. Along with his pension, she'd had sufficient funds to live on. Frugal by nature and nurture, she'd gotten along fine.

Mrs. Entwhistle believed the Bible verse that said the love of money was the root of all evil. She thought it was far better to give it away than become enslaved by it, plus there was the added benefit of having so much fun doing it. Honestly, she couldn't regret having passed along most of her winnings even in the face of this new development. Having too much seemed to make people just as miserable as having too little. The sweet spot was living comfortably without worrying about either scarcity or surplus. But half of Floyd's monthly Social Security check wasn't going to do it. She began a list of options.

Sell the house. It was a seller's market right now, but that would work against her when she went to find a new place. Was it time to consider an over-fifty-five community? Or assisted living? She did NOT need that kind of help just yet, and besides, the monthly cost was ridiculous. It ought to be called a$$i$ted living in her opinion.

She knew Maxine would offer to share her home, but both of them were used to living alone. The worst thing would be to jeopardize a precious friendship through too much togetherness, a chance she was unwilling to take. No, she couldn't live anywhere else as cheaply as she could live in this house where she'd spent her entire adult life. The mortgage had long ago been retired and taxes were low.

Sell possessions. She looked around at the worn furniture, most of it not of the antique variety. Who would want it, let alone pay cash money for it? She owned no important jewelry or sterling silver flatware. She counted the little dog fast asleep at her feet as her most valuable possession. Roger was ancient but he was such a good dog, despite a tendency to flatulence in his old age. An aroma wafted upwards towards Mrs. Entwhistle's nostrils. She waved her hand in front of her face, jerking her thoughts back to the matter at hand.

Get a job. She paused a long time over that one. At seventy-eight, soon to be seventy-nine, it seemed utterly unfeasible. She'd never had a paying job in her life, and the thought of starting now...why, what were her skills, for heaven's sake? She could clean and wash and iron, but nobody was going to hire an old lady to do that. Baby-sitting was appealing; kids fascinated her. Her dear friend, Pete Peters, had three little ones including her namesake, Cora, whom she adored. But then she remembered reality; she'd raised Diane and Tommy and wouldn't exchange that experience for anything, but oh, the work! The rising and kneeling and reaching and carrying! She knew her knees and other parts were simply not up to it.

She was stumped. It was time to call Maxine.

~*~

Maxine was at her door in no time, alerted by the stress in Mrs. Entwhistle's voice.

"Cora, what's wrong?" she demanded from the doorstep. "Don't try to deny it, something's happened. Tell me."

Mrs. Entwhistle did. Maxine's eyes grew rounder and angrier as she listened. At one point she held up her hand to signal she needed a pause and went into the bathroom. Mrs. Entwhistle heard a muffled scream, then Maxine returned serenely to her chair.

"Go on," she said.

When Mrs. Entwhistle got to the end of her short list of options, Maxine nodded. She tapped her fingertips together as she thought. "Getting a job is the best option," she said.

"But Max, I have no skills. Who'd hire me?"

"Nonsense, Cora! You are chock-full of skills. You could give cooking lessons. How many young women know how to make biscuits like yours? You could tutor children in reading, and you'd make it so much fun they'd love it. You could...why, Cora, you could write!"

"Write?"

"Remember when I had my hip replacement operation and you took over my advice column for the *Neighborhood News*? You were a hit. People loved that column."

Maxine sounded wistful. Mrs. Entwhistle knew she'd done a little too well when she filled in for her friend. She hastened to deflect that line of thought.

"They were tickled to have you back. And I couldn't have done it without following your lead, you know that."

"The *Neighborhood News* isn't the answer; it's too small to pay a reporter. But what about the *Pantograph*?"

"The daily paper? Oh, I don't think...."

"Now wait a minute, Cora, let's think it through. The *Pantograph* can't keep help, we know that. They change reporters more than some people change shirts."

"Not exactly a recommendation," Mrs. Entwhistle said.

"No, but the reason nobody stays is the pay is low and the editor, little Jimmy Jack, is a pill."

"Maxine, don't ever go into sales."

"The thing is, you could really do some good at that newspaper. Jimmy Jack isn't the man his father was and he's floundering."

Jimmy Jack's father, James John McNamara, known to one and all as Mac, was the founding editor of the *Pantograph*. He'd started the small daily fifty years ago and built it into a thriving regional newspaper. When he'd suddenly dropped dead during his evening stroll, James John Junior, whom everyone called Jimmy Jack had taken over the family business. He was willing, but like many sons of successful men, he had no fire in his belly for the news business or anything else. Jimmy Jack was indolent, indecisive and ignorant, which Mrs. Entwhistle pointed out.

"He's pleasant, though," Maxine countered. "He could be taught. Mac meant to bring him along, he just died too soon."

"What makes you think Jimmy Jack is looking for help?" Mrs. Entwhistle asked.

"I heard just the other day that he's lost his local beat reporter. Again."

"Local beat...does that mean school board meetings and PTA bake sales? If so, just kill me now."

"You could do it with your eyes closed, Cora. It's people you know talking about the same stuff they've talked about all our lives. You'd go to a few meetings, write your articles here at home, turn them in and collect your paycheck."

"Hmmm." Mrs. Entwhistle had to admit that sounded like something she could do. She'd taught Jimmy Jack in Sunday School when she could cow him with a look; she still had that look. It might work.

"Promise you'll at least go talk to him," Maxine begged.

"Well, I guess I could do that much," Mrs. Entwhistle said. "But do you really think...?"

"I *know* you could do it," Maxine said in a voice that signaled the discussion was over.

Mrs. Entwhistle Rides Again is available on Amazon.

Made in the USA
Coppell, TX
18 April 2021

53969310R00115